THE RIVER HOUSE MYSTERY

Impresario Montague Hammond is scared. He's received threatening, anonymous letters, signed with the drawing of a man hanging from a gallows. And someone has been watching and following him. He invites criminologist Trevor Lowe to his riverside home and requests an investigation. The impresario's star actress Venita Shayne arrives as a houseguest — but she's found strangled in his study the next day. Then, just as Hammond is about to disclose further information to Lowe — he too is murdered . . .

Books by Gerald Verner
in the Linford Mystery Library:

GERALD VERNER

◆

THE
RIVER HOUSE
MYSTERY

Complete and Unabridged

LINFORD
Leicester

First published in Great Britain

First Linford Edition
published 2013

British Library CIP Data

Verner, Gerald.
   The river house mystery. - -
   (Linford mystery library)
   1. Lowe, Trevor (Fictitious character)- -
   Fiction. 2. Detective and mystery stories.
   3. Large type books.
   I. Title II. Series
   823.9'12–dc23

   ISBN 978–1–4448–1475–0

Published by
F. A. Thorpe (Publishing)
Anstey, Leicestershire

Set by Words & Graphics Ltd.
Anstey, Leicestershire
Printed and bound in Great Britain by
T. J. International Ltd., Padstow, Cornwall

This book is printed on acid-free paper

1

A Peculiar Business

Mr. Hammond, that well-known figure in theatrical circles, had recently been disturbed and worried by the receipt of a number of anonymous letters, both threatening and unpleasant, and, since he was a friend of Trevor Lowe's and knew that he liked nothing better than a puzzle to unravel, had come to him to look into the matter rather than risk the possible publicity which would attach if it were put into the hands of the police. At least that is the excuse he offered.

'I'm not taking the threats seriously, of course,' he declared, when he showed the dramatist the half-dozen or so letters he had received. 'But I'm under the impression that somebody's trying to put something across.'

'Have you any idea whom?' inquired Lowe, but Mr. Hammond shook his large head and replied in the negative.

The dramatist was not altogether sure that he was being entirely truthful. He had a vague idea at the back of his mind that Mr. Hammond knew from whom these offensive epistles emanated, and he was confirmed in his view when the producer issued his invitation.

'Come down to Backwaters,' he said. 'I've got several people coming this weekend and you may learn something.'

Lowe would infinitely have preferred not to go, but Mr. Hammond, from long practice, had a persuasive tongue, and when he pleaded that his guests had been specially invited to meet him and included Venita Shayne, the dramatist capitulated.

Of all the stars who blazed in the theatrical firmament at that particular period Venita Shayne was the brightest. Her name dazzled the eye of the beholder in brilliant lights outside the theatre that was fortunate enough to secure her services. Photographs of her in every conceivable pose appeared in the daily and weekly Press with monotonous regularity, and the gossip writers expatiated at length on everything she did.

She was not a particularly good actress, but she was lovely, had personality, and, what was more important, an extremely efficient press agent. Three years before she had been playing small parts in an obscure repertory company touring the provinces, been seen by Mr. Montague Hammond during one of his periodical trips in search of talent, and boosted into her present position of London's most popular and highest paid actress.

The anonymous letters were of the usual kind, scrawled in pencil on dirty scraps of paper, and ranging from the abusive to the definitely threatening. The only thing that lifted them out of the ordinary was the signature. This consisted in every case of a crudely drawn figure dangling at the end of a noose; a childish and inartistic effort, but at the same time, curiously sinister.

Lowe was interested. He had a peculiar intuition that there was something at the back of these scurrilous notes that was definitely serious, and so, since his interest was stronger than his antipathy to house-parties, he resigned himself with a shrug of his shoulders to the upsetting of his plans for a peaceful weekend at his flat, and accompanied by Arnold White drove to Backwaters, reaching the big stone house by the river at a little after four in the afternoon.

Mr. Montague Hammond heard their arrival and came out himself to greet them as White brought the car to a halt in front of the shady porch, his big, fleshy figure clad in spotless flannels.

'Glad you've come, Lowe,' he said, giving the dramatist a flabby handshake. 'We're just having tea on the terrace. I expect you could do with some, or would you prefer a drink?'

'I'd rather have tea,' answered Lowe.

'Have anything you like,' said his host genially. 'Will you come along now, or would you like a wash first?'

'A wash, I think,' said the dramatist.

'Right!' The jovial Mr. Hammond signalled to a manservant who was hovering expectantly in the shadows of the big hall. 'Minter, show Mr. Lowe and his

4

secretary to their rooms.'

The man came silently forward and picked up the two suitcases, which Arnold had deposited on the gravel drive in front of the porch.

'I'll have your car taken round for you to the garage when you come down,' called Mr. Hammond, as they followed the servant up the white enamelled staircase.

* * *

The bedrooms that had been allotted to them were side by side at the end of a corridor, which ran at right angles to the square landing, and both were pleasantly furnished and decorated in restful shades of green. Lowe eyed his approvingly, and when the soft-footed Minter had unpacked their suitcases, showed the bathroom, which was directly opposite, and silently taken his departure, set about removing the dust of the journey from Town.

While he was brushing his hair he glanced out of the open window. A murmur of voices beneath told him that the terrace that his host had mentioned lay immediately below. By leaning forward slightly he could see a broad flight of shallow steps that descended to a rose-garden. Beyond that a smooth stretch of grass sloped gently to the riverbank, dotted with ornamental trees and flowering shrubs and brightened with gaily-cushioned chairs.

Through the drooping willows that fringed its edge he could see the placid surface of the stream, which was a backwater of the main river and probably gave the house its name. A motor-launch was moored to a little white-painted landing stage from which a diving board projected, and further along a couple of punts and a dinghy were just visible by a clump of bushes.

In the shimmering heat of the late August afternoon the picture was pleasantly cool and peaceful.

He finished brushing his hair and went in search of White.

They descended the stairs and found Minter waiting for them in the hall below. The servant escorted them to a big, low-ceilinged lounge, through a pair of wide French windows to a loggia on which four people were lounging in wicker chairs, grouped haphazardly round a table set with tea things. As they appeared Montague Hammond hoisted his large bulk with difficulty out of his chair and came towards them.

'Come along, Lowe,' he cried heartily. 'There's a chair over there. Make yourself at home. That's my wife, and this is Marjorie Lovelace — you've heard of her, of course — and that's John Moore.' He waved a fat hand vaguely towards the group.

'Very pleased to meet you, Mr. Lowe,' said a thin woman by the tea table. 'You'll be glad of some tea after your journey, I expect.'

The dramatist murmured a polite affirmative as he dropped into the chair indicated. There was something about Mrs. Hammond that rather jarred. Her hair was too obviously dyed; the paint on her lips had been supplied by a too lavish and inartistic hand; the dress she was wearing was too frilly; the voice a little harsh ... Swiftly he made a mental catalogue of her defects.

She poured out the tea and Lowe accepted his cup with a word of thanks. As he sipped the refreshing beverage he took stock of the other two members of the party.

Marjorie Lovelace he knew by reputation as a very competent small-part actress. She was a pretty, dark girl, with the blue-black hair and violet eyes that betrayed her Irish origin.

John Moore was a very ordinary type. The usual good-looking young actor. A visit to any theatrical agent's office would produce a hundred John Moores at the shortest possible notice.

'Venita isn't coming down until later,' said Mr. Hammond. 'Eric Norman's driving her down in time for dinner.'

Mrs. Hammond was handing White his tea as her husband spoke and Lowe saw her face change. Her thin, carefully pencilled brows drew together in a frown and her straight lips tightened. The expression was fleeting. It was gone in a moment, but while it lasted it had been

8

entirely disapproving. Mrs. Hammond obviously did not like the famous Venita, or was it Eric Norman of whom she disapproved?

'That's her press agent, isn't it?' asked Lowe.

Hammond nodded.

'Yes. Brilliant chap,' he answered. 'Venita owes a lot to him.'

Marjorie Lovelace sighed and stretched her slim legs.

'Does one have to be able to act to achieve success?' she remarked, 'or is it only necessary to acquire a brilliant press agent?'

Mr. Hammond chuckled throatily.

'Now, Marjorie,' he said, waving a podgy finger warningly, 'don't be catty. Nobody can say that Venita is a bad actress.'

'Nobody can say she's a good one!' snapped Mrs. Hammond acidly. 'She can play one kind of part and that's all.'

Her husband laughed.

'That's enough,' he replied, 'so long as there are authors who write that one kind of part for her.'

'A good actress should be able to play anything!' said his wife. 'Don't you agree, Mr. Lowe?'

Trevor Lowe set down his empty cup.

'If that was the accepted standard,' he remarked, 'then there are no good actresses on the English stage.'

'That's rather a sweeping statement,' said Marjorie Lovelace. 'Why don't you qualify it by saying the West End stage?'

'I don't see why an actor or an actress shouldn't specialise in one kind of part,' put in John Moore languidly. His voice was carefully modulated, but he rather over-stressed his sibilants. 'After all, other professions are full of people who make a speciality of one thing. There are specialists for nerve trouble and specialists for throat trouble, and specialists for cancer, in the medical profession. Writers specialise in one particular subject. You wouldn't call a man a bad author because he only writes one particular type of story.'

'I should call him a bad author,' said Lowe, 'if he *could* only write one particular type of story.'

'Well, well,' said Mr. Hammond.

10

'Whether Venita's a bad or a good actress doesn't matter a damn, she's box-office. That's the thing that counts. The public adore her and her name in lights outside a theatre means seventy-five per cent towards the success of the play.'

'Naturally you'd stick up for her,' said Mrs. Hammond with a sneer, 'seeing that she's a protégée of yours.'

'She's put a lot of money in my pocket,' said her husband good-humouredly, 'and I'm always ready to stick up for people who do that.'

'Mostly due to her press agent,' muttered Marjorie Lovelace, but she said it in so low a voice that only Lowe, who was sitting next to her, heard the words. It was not what she said but the vindictiveness in her tone that surprised him.

2

Venita Shayne

Venita Shayne and Eric Norman arrived at seven o'clock. Lowe was introduced to them when he came down after dressing for dinner. He had seen the girl from the other side of the footlights, but this was the first time he had met her in the flesh, and he had to admit that she looked even lovelier off the stage than she did on.

She was a natural platinum blonde with a complexion that owed very little to artifice, and although only of medium height she looked taller because of her slimness. Her eyes, large and fringed with unusually long lashes, were of a rather rare shade of blue, so deep that it almost amounted to violet.

'I've been wanting to meet you for such a long time, Mr. Lowe,' she said conventionally, in her soft, slightly husky voice, as she held out her hand and let her cool

12

fingers rest for a moment in his palm. 'I've seen all your plays and adored them.'

'That's very nice of you, Miss Shayne,' murmured Lowe. 'I saw you play a few weeks ago and thought you were excellent.'

'Of course she's excellent!' said Eric Norman in his deep voice. 'Venita Shayne is never anything else.'

She looked up at him with the childish, half whimsical smile that her public paid nightly to see. The newspapers called Venita Shayne the most beautiful woman in England, and when she smiled the description was almost true.

'As my press agent you couldn't very well say anything else, could you, Eric?' she remarked, and he grinned.

Lowe liked him. His rugged face was pleasant and his shrewd grey eyes hinted at a more than usual intelligence.

The rest of the party joined them on the loggia, and presently Minter appeared with a tray of cocktails. They chatted gaily, mostly about plays and the theatre, until the servant appeared again to announce that dinner was served.

The meal was a pleasant one, perfectly

cooked and perfectly served. Looking back on it later Trevor Lowe remembered two items that stood out vividly in his mind. The first occurred while Venita was relating a tit-bit of scandal concerning a well-known M.P. and the daughter of a duke.

Lowe listened politely although the recital was not particularly interesting to him, for he knew neither of the parties concerned except by repute. He was sitting opposite Venita, and allowing his eyes to stray away from her vivacious face turned his gaze towards his hostess.

Mrs. Hammond, at the bottom of the table, was peeling a peach, and although her fingers were busy her eyes were fixed on Venita Shayne. They were half hidden by the lids, but not hidden enough to conceal the hatred which grew slowly from a spark in their depths to a blaze of devouring fire. Never in his life had Lowe seen such a blaze of passionate dislike. The next moment she saw that he was watching her and dropped her eyes to her plate.

The second incident occurred almost

immediately after. Venita had finished her story and was nibbling at a grape. Her eyes were very bright and her face a little flushed, for she had drunk quite a lot of the champagne that Mr. Hammond had so lavishly provided. Suddenly she turned her head and looked at her host.

'I've got a surprise for you,' she said. 'In fact I think it will be a surprise to everyone who knows me. I'm engaged to be married!'

Montague dropped his fruit knife with a clatter and stared at the girl, his large mouth drooping open foolishly.

'Engaged to be married?' he echoed, when he was capable of speech.

She nodded, and Lowe thought she was rather pleased at the sensation she had created.

'Yes, I thought you'd be surprised,' she said.

'When did this happen, Venita?' asked Eric Norman, and there was an edge to his voice.

'This morning,' she answered.

'And you never told me!' he said reproachfully. 'If you'd let me know at once I could have got it in the evening papers.'

'I don't want it in the papers — at least, not yet,' she said. 'It's to be more or less a secret at present.'

'Who's the lucky man?' demanded Norman, 'or is that a secret too?'

'Well — ' she hesitated. 'It's Harold Cavendish,' she said after a pause.

Lowe raised his eyebrows slightly. The Honourable Harold Cavendish was the only son of Lord Glenriven, one of the largest landholders in England and a member of the richest and oldest family in the country. Venita Shayne had certainly done very well for herself.

'And I can't publish it?' said Eric Norman, and groaned extravagantly when she shook her head. 'The best piece of publicity for a month and it's got to be kept dark. It's — it's criminal!'

He spoke lightly, but underneath his lightness the dramatist thought he saw a very real annoyance.

'Perhaps Miss Shayne doesn't want it to become public in case she has to deny it later,' said Mrs. Hammond a little venomously.

Venita reddened.

'What do you mean by that?' she began angrily. 'D'you think — ?'

'I know what these kind of engagements are,' interrupted the thin woman with a sniff. 'On one day and off the next!'

'Well, this one won't be!' declared Venita. 'And I think it's beastly of you to suggest — '

'Eva was only joking, Venita,' interposed Montague Hammond, shooting a sharp, angry glance at his wife. 'Don't take any notice of her. I congratulate you, my dear, though I hope it won't mean your leaving the stage.'

'I'm afraid it will, Monty,' said the girl. 'But not yet, anyway.'

'Well, good luck to you,' said Mr. Hammond. 'It won't make any difference to your playing in my new show, anyhow.'

'No, I'm looking forward to that,' she replied with a smile.

There was a murmur of good wishes and congratulations from everybody, with the exception of Mrs. Hammond, who stared at her plate with hard eyes and tight lips. Then the subject was dropped.

3

Murder!

The morning of that fatal Saturday gave promise that the day to follow would be even hotter than the previous one. When Lowe awoke a little before seven there was a blue haze over the opposite bank of the river, and already it was uncomfortably warm.

He had slept well, an unusual thing for him to do in a strange bed, and it was therefore all the more unaccountable that he should have felt so heavy and depressed. It was unlike him to feel like this in the morning, for as a rule that was the time when he was at his brightest. He put it down to a touch of liver, caused, no doubt, by the richness of the food he had consumed on the previous night.

He stood for some time at the open window contemplating the beauty of the morning, and gradually that sense of

18

weight at his heart wore off.

He was considering making his way to the bathroom when there came a rap on the door and a maid entered with a tray of morning tea. Sitting on the side of his bed he drank the tea leisurely, and ate one of the accompanying rusks. When he had smoked a cigarette he set about the business of shaving and dressing.

It was eight o'clock when he came down, and apparently none of the rest of the household was yet up. Leaving the house through the open windows of the lounge he strolled down to the edge of the water. It was very clear and there was scarcely any current. Scores of small fish were darting to and fro, giving an occasional splash of silver as they turned sideways and caught the light of the sun.

He was still watching them interestedly when he was joined by Montague Hammond. The producer looked as though he had had a bad night. There were bags beneath his eyes and his fat face was grey and unhealthy looking. He greeted Lowe cheerily enough, however.

'Lovely morning, isn't it?' he said.

'Hope you slept well.'

'Excellently!' answered the dramatist truthfully.

'That's good!' said Mr. Hammond. 'Most people do, you know, down here. It's the river air. Bit relaxing. I'd like to have a talk with you after breakfast about those things. I had another this morning, rather different from the rest.'

He took an envelope from his pocket, addressed in badly printed capitals. His name was spelt with one M and Backwaters had been made into two words.

'What do you think of it?' he asked, as Lowe withdrew the single sheet of paper and stared at the message. It ran:

'You watch out. There's trouble coming and it's coming soon. That girl's for it, the blonde one, and others will follow.'

Below was the roughly executed drawing of the dangling man.

'What do you make of it?' repeated Hammond, and Lowe shook his head.

'It obviously refers to Miss Shayne,' he answered.

'That's what I thought.' The producer nodded and frowned. 'I'd give a lot to know what's behind these things, Lowe, and who sends them.'

'You've no idea?' asked the dramatist, looking him straight in the eye.

'No. You've asked me that before,' grunted Hammond, avoiding his gaze. 'If I had any idea I'd hand him over to the police. It's a stupid thing to do.'

At that moment Minter came out to inform them that breakfast was ready, and they strolled back to the house. The meal had been set on the loggia, and Arnold, John Moore and Marjorie Lovelace were already seated at the table. Lowe learned that Venita Shayne and Mrs. Hammond were having breakfast in bed. Marjorie Lovelace, looking very cool and pretty in white, poured out the coffee for them.

When the meal was over Hammond carried the dramatist off to his study, leaving the others to their own devices.

He waved Lowe into one of the armchairs, settled his large bulk comfortably in the swing chair before the desk, and unlocking a drawer produced a box of cigars.

'Try one,' he said, holding it out. 'I can recommend them.'

The dramatist carefully chose one of the brown cylinders, lit it and blew out a cloud of fragrant smoke.

'Like it?' asked Mr. Hammond.

'It's excellent!' said Lowe. 'But you didn't bring me in here to get my judgment on your cigars.'

A troubled look crossed the face of the producer.

'No, you're right. I didn't,' he admitted. 'I'm worried, Lowe. Very worried.'

'About these anonymous letters?' said the dramatist.

'Well, yes, partly.' The producer fiddled with the cigar, which he had taken out, but refrained from lighting. 'Not altogether.'

He stopped abruptly, and there was an awkward silence.

'Listen, Hammond,' said Lowe. 'You've got something on your mind. You've had it on your mind for a long time. When you came to me about these letters you were receiving that wasn't the only reason. There was something else.'

'How in the world did you know that?' Mr. Hammond's large face was expressive of astonishment.

'It was obvious,' said the dramatist. 'It was partly the reason why I agreed to look into the matter for you. Now come along, be quite frank with me. Tell me what's bothering you.'

'Well, if you want to know I'm — scared!' muttered Hammond

'Why?' inquired Lowe.

'For — well, for various reasons.' The other appeared to find difficulty in expressing himself. 'You'll probably laugh, but quite a number of queer things have occurred recently.'

'What sort of queer things?' Lowe was definitely interested.

'Well, for one,' said Hammond, 'I'm being watched.'

'Watched?' The dramatist took his cigar from between his lips and eyed his host inquiringly. 'By whom?'

'That's the trouble,' said Hammond. 'I don't know. I'll give you an instance. The other night I was invited to a supper party by one of the people playing in my theatre. I had some business to do and I was one of the last to leave the building. There was a man standing near the stage door and I thought he looked at me rather keenly as I passed. I thought no more about it and went to the party. At three o'clock in the morning I was getting into my car when I saw the same man. He was standing in the shadows near the entrance to the block of flats which I'd just come out of.'

'You're sure it was the same man?' asked Lowe.

'Positive!' declared Mr. Hammond. 'A week ago while my wife was away a punt moored up to the island opposite and a man in it began fishing. He spent almost the whole day there. He never caught anything, but I saw his face, and it was the same man. I've seen him on several other occasions lurking near the entrance to this house, and outside my offices.'

'And you've no idea who he is?' said the dramatist.

'Not the slightest!' answered the producer. 'Coming on the top of these letters it's — well, it's a little unnerving.'

'Have you any enemies?' said Lowe, and Hammond shrugged his shoulders.

'Who hasn't?' he answered. 'I suppose I've made one or two during my time, but I can't think of any, well, serious ones.'

'What makes you think this is serious?' said the dramatist.

'I don't know.' Montague Hammond's face was grave and he shook his head. 'It's — you can call it an instinct or a hunch, or whatever you like. It amounts to the same thing. I've just got a feeling that there's something — something very unpleasant brewing. It was partly because I wanted to have this talk with you, Lowe, that I invited you down. I know how keen you are on mysteries.'

He changed the subject abruptly and launched forth enthusiastically on a description of his new play, and Lowe was left with the impression that he had not said what he had intended saying, at least not all he had intended saying.

He wished later that he had pressed Montague Hammond further, but by then his wish was useless.

Luncheon was served on the terrace,

and it was a pleasant meal. Venita Shayne was in high spirits and even Mrs. Hammond seemed to have lost some of her acidity of the previous night. There was no trace of the peculiar atmosphere that had been present after the girl's announcement of her engagement.

'Do any of you people know anything about watches?' she asked during a lull in the conversation.

'Why?' said Eric Norman, looking across at her.

'Because something's gone wrong with mine,' she explained. 'It's stopped. It was all right last night, but when I put it on this morning it wouldn't go.'

'Let's have a look at it,' he said.

She took the tiny jewelled timepiece from her wrist and passed it across to him. With knitted brows he examined it.

'Stopped at two o'clock this morning,' he muttered, and uttered a low whistle. 'Look,' he said. 'The back's dented. Badly, too. You must have hit it against something. Only a jeweller can put that right.'

He handed it back to her and she replaced it on her wrist.

'You won't need it here,' said the producer. 'There are plenty of clocks about. Now then, what would you people like to do this afternoon?'

'I've got some letters I must write,' said Venita. 'I hate writing letters, but it must be done.'

'You can use my study,' said Hammond. 'You'll find everything you want there, notepaper, envelopes and stamps. Now, what about you other people?'

His wife suggested bridge — Lowe discovered later that this was a passion of hers — and Marjorie Lovelace, John Moore and Hammond hailed the suggestion with delight.

'You can count me out,' said Norman. 'I loathe the game, and I'm a bad player, anyway.'

'And me,' put in the dramatist. 'I think I'll just make myself comfortable in one of those seductive-looking chairs and do nothing!'

'I'll come and talk to you when I've finished my letters,' said Venita. 'It's too hot to do anything but sit about and doze. What are you going to do, Eric?'

'Read,' answered Norman promptly. 'I'm in the middle of a rattling good thriller and I want to finish it.'

He accompanied Venita into the house to fetch his book from his bedroom, and Lowe strolled down to the lawn to find a comfortable chair in which he could laze away the afternoon. He found one and installed himself among the cushions with a sigh of contentment Lighting a cigarette, he watched through half-closed eyes the others making preparations for their game.

Minter brought a card table and set it in the shade of one of the willows. While he was collecting chairs from the terrace Eric Norman reappeared with a book in his hand. He came down and settled himself a few yards away from Lowe and began to read. Hammond went in to collect the cards and scoring tablets and the bridge party settled down to their game.

Lowe threw away the end of his cigarette and glanced at his watch with a yawn. It was a quarter to three.

The heat was stifling. The sun poured

down from a cloudless sky and there was not a breath of wind. The drowsy hum of bees and the soft ripple of the water as a girl in a canoe paddled slowly past were the only sounds that broke the stillness.

Arnold White, who lay sprawling on the grass near the water's edge, rose to his feet and stretched himself.

'I think I'll go for a trip in one of the punts,' he said. 'Care to come?'

Half asleep his employer shook his head. His lunch, and the oppressive heat combined, made him feel drowsy. He was nodding when he heard the sound of excited voices and looked up quickly.

For a moment he thought it was a row among the bridge players but twisting round in his chair he discovered that it was Minter and Mr. Hammond. The servant, his face white and glistening, was speaking rapidly and shrilly to the stout man. He heard Hammond say: 'My God! I'll come at once!' and out of the corner of his eye saw Eric Norman drop his book and hastily rise to his feet.

Wondering what had happened he got up quickly and went over to the startled group. Their faces told him it was something serious before he put his question to Hammond.

'It's Venita!' muttered the Producer hoarsely, his face the colour of chalk. 'She — she — !'

'What's happened to Venita?' Eric Norman snapped the question as he joined them.

'She's been taken ill or something,' answered Montague Hammond. 'I — ' He broke off as with a muttered exclamation Norman went striding towards the house.

Lowe followed with Minter, the agitated Mr. Hammond waddling along in the rear.

'What has happened?' asked the dramatist.

The white-faced servant licked his lips.

'I don't know, sir. Something rather dreadful, I'm afraid,' he answered shakily. 'Miss Shayne is either — ill — or dead!'

'Dead!' echoed Lowe.

The man nodded and swallowed with difficulty.

'Yes,' he said huskily. 'She's — she's huddled up on the desk — in Mr.

Hammond's study — she wouldn't answer when I spoke to her. She wouldn't move when I touched her . . . '

They crossed the loggia and hurried through the coolness of the lounge. Norman was halfway up the stairs before they reached the hall, and they followed him to the door of the study on the first floor. It was half open. As he reached it Lowe saw Norman by the desk and heard the sharp, horrified intake of his breath. He looked up sharply with a haggard face as the dramatist entered.

'My God! Look here!' he said in a harsh voice, a voice that was so totally unlike his own as to be unrecognisable.

Lowe looked, and his own face changed colour. In the swivel chair by the big writing table sat Venita Shayne. One arm hung limply down by her side, the other, bare to the elbow, was flung out across the blotting pad. Between them rested the platinum head, twisted half sideways . . .

Lowe came to Norman's side, and as he reached it he saw what it was that had caused that horrified intake of breath, for now the face was visible.

31

The eyes were wide and staring and suffused with blood; the fair skin blotched and mottled and of a horrible livid colour . . . One glance was sufficient to tell him the truth.

Venita Shayne, beautiful no longer, was dead! And the savage fingers that had pressed out her life had left marks that stood out cruelly against the whiteness of her throat.

4

The Circular Mark

'Don't touch her!' said Trevor Lowe sharply as Eric Norman made a movement towards the sprawling figure of the dead actress. 'Nothing must be touched until the police have seen her!'

'The police!' The hoarse croak came from Montague Hammond in the open doorway. 'What do you mean, Lowe?'

'The police must be sent for at once!' interrupted the dramatist sternly. 'This is murder!'

The ominous word sent a little ripple of sound like the sighing of an expiring breath over the group by the door.

'Murder!' breathed Hammond. 'But — how can it be murder? Nobody could have — we were all outside — !'

'All the same it's murder!' said Lowe. 'She's been strangled, and she couldn't have strangled herself.' He looked at the telephone, which stood on a corner of the desk. 'Shall I telephone or will you?' he inquired.

Hammond passed a shaking hand across his damp forehead.

'You telephone,' he muttered huskily. 'Good Heavens! This is dreadful! Venita! Poor little Venita!' His voice choked as he stared at the pathetic figure in the chair, bathed in the full glare of the afternoon sun.

Lowe lifted the telephone from its rack, and after a short delay was connected with the police station. Rapidly and without waste of words he explained what had happened, answered a few questions that were put to him, and putting the instrument back, turned to the others.

'The police are coming at once,' he said gravely.

'I can't believe it!' Montague Hammond was still staring at the crouching figure by the desk as though, by the very intensity of his gaze, he would instil life into that motionless body. 'She was always so — so *alive*!' His voice cracked and his thick lips quivered.

Eric Norman said nothing. Since Lowe had checked that first spasmodic movement he had remained rigid, his rugged face expressionless, his eyes fixed on the livid face of the dead girl with a peculiar fascination.

Lowe touched Hammond on the arm.

'Come,' he said kindly. 'Pull yourself together. It's a dreadful thing to have happened, but it's no good letting it get you down.'

The producer stared at him dumbly and there was pain in the brown eyes.

'Who could have done it?' he whispered. 'Who could have done it?'

Lowe was asking himself the same question without discovering a satisfactory answer.

'That remains to be found out,' he said. 'Go and take your wife and the others away.' He glanced towards the white faces in the doorway.

Hammond nodded, but made no effort to move. He seemed reluctant to leave that room to which death had come in its most dreadful form.

'Go on, Hammond.' It was Eric

Norman who spoke and his voice was level and emotionless. 'You can do no good here. None of us can do any good.'

The stout man nodded again slowly and Lowe thought he looked a curiously pathetic figure as he stood there hesitant and obviously grief-stricken.

'No,' he swallowed with difficulty, 'I suppose — suppose you're right. We can't do anything, can we?' He moved unsteadily like a drunken man towards the door. 'Come on, Eva. Come on, Marjorie,' he muttered. 'We'll go downstairs.' He pushed them gently away in front of him, and then with an abrupt movement pulled the door to.

'He's pretty cut up, isn't he?' remarked Norman when he had gone.

'It's not surprising,' said Lowe, bending over the desk and examining its neatly arranged appointments. 'She was a protégée of his and he was practically entirely responsible for her success. It must have given him a terrible shock.'

'It was generally supposed that she was more than a protégée,' said Norman significantly.

'Whether there's any truth in that or not,' said the dramatist coldly, 'it doesn't seem to me to be the best time to choose for discussing it.'

Norman reddened angrily and then went white.

'You're quite right,' he muttered. 'I shouldn't have said that.'

He relapsed into silence, watching the other as he peered about among the objects on the top of the desk. Apparently he found something that interested him, for suddenly he bent forward in an attitude of concentration, and then looked round quickly.

'You must have received a lot of letters from Miss Shayne during the time you acted as her press agent,' he said.

A little surprised, Norman nodded.

'A good number,' he answered.

'You'll be able to tell me then,' went on Lowe, 'whether it was a habit of hers to put the time and day instead of the date at the head of her paper?'

'Yes, it was,' replied Norman curiously. 'Why?'

'There's a freshly started letter here,'

explained the dramatist.

'You can just see it under her right hand. No, don't touch anything!' He laid a restraining hand on the other's arm as he came around to his side. 'Look, there! It's headed: Saturday, 3.15.'

He showed the press agent the partly visible sheet of notepaper with the dead girl's sprawling writing.

'Yes, Venita always started her letters like that,' said Norman. 'What about it?'

'It may be very important,' said Lowe gravely. 'You see it proves she was alive at a quarter past three.'

'Well, supposing she was — ' began Norman impatiently, and then, realising what the other meant, 'By Jove! You mean she must have been killed between three-fifteen and — !'

'The time Minter found her,' finished Lowe. 'Which was roughly a quarter to four.'

'In that case,' exclaimed Norman excitedly, 'unless Minter himself or one of the servants killed her — and that's a ridiculous supposition — some stranger must have done it, because everybody else was on the lawn by the river from three o'clock onwards.'

Lowe nodded.

'You see now how important the time on that letter's going to be?' he said.

'Yes,' agreed Norman. 'Half a minute, though,' he added, as something struck him. 'Perhaps Venita made a mistake in the time. D'you remember she said her watch went wrong at lunch — ?'

Lowe pointed to the silver clock, which was ticking steadily a few inches away from the dead girl's head.

'She couldn't have made a mistake,' he answered quietly, 'whatever had happened to her watch. She had that in front of her, and it's dead right.'

'But nobody in the house *could* have done it,' said Norman.

'Apparently.' The dramatist was staring down at the dead girl's extended arm, flung out across the blotting pad.

'What are you looking at?' asked Norman interestedly.

'This,' said Lowe, and pointed to a small red, circular mark that stood out vividly on the white flesh.

'It looks like a cigarette burn,' said Norman, staring curiously.

'It wasn't there at lunch,' muttered the dramatist, frowning, 'I'm certain of that.'

'Perhaps the murderer was smoking a cigarette,' suggested Norman, 'and she got the burn in the struggle.'

'Perhaps,' said Lowe, but his tone was doubtful. 'I'm not so sure that it is a cigarette burn. There's no blackening.'

He stared at the mark with pursed lips, his brows drawn together, and then, as a sharp knocking rang through the house, he straightened up.

'That will be the police,' he said.

5

The Invisible Killer

Inspector Cotter of the Berkshire Constabulary was a thin, shrewd-faced man, with a weather-beaten complexion and small, twinkling black eyes. He was accompanied by a sergeant, a stolid-looking constable, and a youngish, fair-haired man whom Lowe rightly guessed to be the doctor.

He listened while the dramatist briefly told him what had occurred, took a quick look at the body, and clicked his teeth.

'It seems to be a nasty business, sir,' he said presently. 'A very nasty business indeed. There's no doubt about this being murder, if course. I'm very glad to meet you, Mr. Lowe.' His bird-like eyes fixed themselves on the dramatist. 'You've had a lot to do with this sort of thing. What d'you make of this affair?'

Lowe shrugged his shoulders.

'I don't make anything of it at all,' he

declared. 'Except that the crime was apparently committed by some person who entered the house while the household were outside.'

'Why do you say that, sir?' asked Cotter.

The dramatist showed him the newly started letter.

'I see.' The inspector pursed his lips. 'This appears to mean that everyone has an alibi, with the exception of the servants.'

Lowe nodded.

'I suppose,' — a sudden thought seemed to have occurred to Cotter — 'that it is Miss Shayne's writing — ?'

'There's no doubt about that,' broke in Eric Norman. 'I've got a letter from her in my room. You can compare the two if you like.'

'Thank you, sir. I should like to,' said the inspector. 'I was just wondering, Mr. Lowe,' he went on, when the press agent left the room, 'if someone hadn't been clever — '

'Faked an alibi, you mean?' finished the dramatist. 'The same idea occurred to me, Inspector, but that sprawling writing would be difficult to imitate. No, I'm pretty sure she began that letter herself.'

Cotter scratched his chin.

'In that case it looks as if it's going to be a difficult business,' the remarked. 'Will you have a look at her now, Doctor?'

He addressed the fair-haired man, who gave a quick nod and came over to the desk. While he was making his examination Eric Norman returned, carrying in his hand a folded sheet of paper which he gave to the inspector. The comparison between the note addressed to Eric Norman and the writing on the freshly started letter left no room for doubt. The writing was identical.

'No argument about that,' muttered the inspector, and Lowe agreed. 'I'll keep this, if you don't mind, sir,' he said, and when Norman nodded, folded the paper and put it carefully away in his large wallet. As he returned this to his pocket the doctor looked up from his unpleasant task.

'Well, I've finished!' he said curtly. 'Death was caused by strangulation.

There'll be an autopsy, of course, but there's no doubt of that.'

'The strangler must have been pretty quiet,' remarked Cotter. 'There isn't any sign of a struggle.'

'There wouldn't be,' replied the doctor briefly. 'She was unconscious when she was strangled!'

'Unconscious!' The exclamation came from Lowe.

'Yes. Look here.' The doctor skilfully parted the pale hair at the top of the head. A livid bruise showed through on the skin of the skull. 'She was struck with some heavy instrument, not enough to break the bone but sufficient to cause a contusion and immediate unconsciousness. After that, of course, it was a simple matter.'

The inspector fingered his chin and frowned.

'I wonder what she was struck with?' he muttered, and Lowe, who had been glancing quickly round the room, pointed to a bronze statuette that stood on the mantelpiece.

'How about that?' he suggested, and

44

the doctor swung round.

'Yes, that might have been the weapon,' he said. 'That, or something similar.'

'About how long has she been dead?' asked the inspector.

'As nearly as I can say, two hours,' was the reply. 'It might be less, it might be a little more. It's impossible to be accurate within half an hour or so.'

Cotter glanced at the desk clock. It was almost exactly five.

'That would fit in,' he said, looking at Lowe.

The dramatist nodded.

'What do you make of that mark on her arm, Doctor?' he asked.

The police surgeon peered at it and wrinkled his brows.

'It's very slight,' he said. 'A burn of some sort.'

'Would you say it was recent?' inquired Lowe.

'Yes,' was the answer. 'Quite recent.'

Cotter looked at him quickly.

'D'you think it's important, sir?' he inquired.

'I don't know whether it's important or

not,' answered Lowe slowly. 'It certainly puzzles me. It wasn't there the last time I saw Miss Shayne alive, and that was just before she entered the house after lunch with the intention of coming in here to write her letters.'

'I don't see how it can have any bearing on this business — ' began the inspector doubtfully.

'I don't say that it has,' broke in Lowe. 'But it's curious all the same. I'm always interested in things that are unaccountable, and that burn, at the moment, is unaccounted for.'

'Most likely it was caused by a cigarette,' said Cotter, who was obviously not very interested in the mark on the dead woman's arm. He sighed. 'Well, I suppose I'd better get busy.'

The routine work attaching to wilful murder is infinite. The photographers arrived, and photographs of the room and the dead actress were taken from several angles, and only when this was done did the inspector permit the pathetic remains to be moved and transferred to the waiting ambulance.

Every object in the study was tested for fingerprints, after which Cotter took the statements of the various members of the household, but they were not very helpful. One thing, however, was proved, which, instead of making the mystery clearer, only rendered it more puzzling.

The evidence of the housemaid, combined with that of Minter, showed conclusively that no stranger could have entered Backwaters at the time the crime was committed. The housemaid had been feeling the heat and had strolled down the drive to the gate leading on to the main road. She had been there from a quarter to three till nearly half-past, and no one had entered. There was a high stone wall surrounding Mr. Hammond's establishment on the land side and this was topped with broken glass and was practically unclimbable. Had, however, anyone succeeded in scaling this obstacle and reaching the house they could not have found their way to the study without passing Minter who, from three o'clock onwards, had been in the hall.

It was the ringing of the telephone bell

that had caused the tragic discovery.

When he had first heard it he concluded that as Miss Shayne was occupying the study at the time she would answer it. When it continued to ring he thought perhaps she had gone up to her room. Going upstairs he had found her — dead. This was at approximately half-past three. He had seen nobody and had not expected to see anyone, since the entire household were out on the lawn which ran down to the riverbank.

Inspector Cotter questioned him regarding the telephone call, hoping that this might supply some kind of a clue, but his hopes were dashed, for it turned out that the call had merely been a wrong number.

Neither was there anything of value to be learned from the rest of the people at Backwaters. When Eric Norman had accompanied Venita into the house he had left her at the door of Montague Hammond's study and had not seen her again alive. The only other person who had entered the house during the time Venita was in the study was Hammond himself. This had been just before a quarter to three, when he had gone to collect the cards and scoring blocks for the bridge game.

No one had moved from the lawn between five minutes to three and the time Minter had made his discovery, therefore, since Venita could not have been killed, on the evidence of the letter, until after three-fifteen, it was impossible for any member of the household to have committed the crime.

It was equally impossible, or nearly so, for any stranger to has done so, and this was the problem Lowe and the inspector were faced with at nine o'clock on that Saturday night when they had completed their investigations.

'It's a complete facer, sir,' Cotter confided, when they talked it over in the study. 'A complete facer! So far as the evidence goes nobody strangled the girl!'

'Then somewhere the evidence lies,' said the dramatist. 'She couldn't have strangled herself. Did you find any prints?'

The inspector shook his head,

'None of any use,' he declared. 'There were plenty of Mr. Hammond's, as one might expect, and one or two of Miss Shayne's, the housemaid's and Minter's, but nobody else's.'

'None on the bronze statuette?' inquired Lowe.

'No,' said Cotter, shaking his head again. 'None at all! But there was a fair hair sticking to the head of the figure, so I don't think there's any doubt that it was used to stun the girl as she sat at the desk.'

'It's queer, that,' muttered Trevor Lowe. 'Surely she'd hardly have allowed a stranger to walk up behind her without making any attempt to give the alarm? And if she'd cried out, Minter, who was in the hall, would have heard her.'

'Perhaps she wasn't aware there was anyone in the room, sir,' said Cotter.

'But she must have been!' answered the dramatist. 'Nobody could walk to the mantelpiece, pick up the statuette, and come back to the desk while she was sitting there without her being aware of it, unless the killer was invisible.'

'Well, there it is,' said the inspector wearily. The intense heat of his exertions had made him a very tired man. 'As it stands it's an impossibility.'

Lowe agreed with him, for in truth it was. Yet there must be the explanation, something that they had overlooked.

At ten o'clock Inspector Cotter and his sergeant departed, leaving the constable on guard with an order that no one should leave the house without permission from the police.

The tragedy had not unnaturally left a shadow an atmosphere of depression. Dinner had been a silent meal, the end of which everyone had welcomed with relief.

Lowe was anxious to question Montague Hammond concerning the dead woman's past, but the producer was still in a dazed condition, and out of sympathetic consideration for him the dramatist decided to postpone what could only be an unpleasant ordeal. He was sorry after that he had allowed his sympathies to intervene.

Arnold White had been acquainted of the tragedy on his return from his river trip, and when the rest of the household had retired, which they did early, he came to Lowe's room.

'Have you discovered anything?' he asked, as he closed the door. His employer shook his head.

'No, nothing,' he answered.

'I've been wondering,' said Arnold, perching himself on the edge of the bed, 'whether there's any connection between Miss Shayne's death and those anonymous letters.'

'I've been wondering the same,' said Lowe. 'That last one which Hammond received this morning hinted at something of the sort.' He had said nothing to the inspector concerning the scurrilous notes or Montague Hammond's apprehension, which they had apparently induced. They might have nothing to do with the murder, and he wanted time to consider the matter before taking Cotter into his confidence.

'It's a puzzling business,' muttered the secretary, frowning. 'So far as I can see nobody can have killed the girl.'

'Well, she *was* killed,' said Lowe, 'and so somebody killed her. Though who he was and how he managed it I'll admit I haven't the faintest idea.'

They discussed the matter at some length, but arrived at no satisfactory conclusion. Presently Arnold went off to bed, leaving Lowe alone. Making himself comfortable in a dressing gown he pulled a chair to the open window, for the night was unpleasantly hot, and tried to sort out his impressions.

That mark on the girl's arm fascinated him. At the back of his mind was a conviction that it had a bearing on her death, but for the life of him he couldn't see how. In his mind's eye he conjured up a picture of the study, visualising the desk and its contents. Near the telephone, he remembered, was a large ashtray, and this had been clean. The girl therefore, had not been smoking, which tended to confirm the fact that the burn had not been caused by a cigarette. Her murderer might have been, but there was no cigarette end in the fireplace, nor in another part of the room. He had taken particular note of this. The study was fitted with an electric fire and the hearth was clean. It was hardly likely, also, that the person who had killed Venita would have kept the cigarette alight between his lips while he strangled the girl.

What was there on the desk that might have caused that mark? The telephone stood on the right-hand corner. Near it was the ashtray. Beside that a water-bottle and glass. Then there was a rack of reference books, an onyx pen-stand holding fountain-pens and a stationery rack. On the left was the clock. That, together with the big, leather-bound blotter and a calendar, was all. There was not even a desk-lighter. Nothing, in fact, that could have supplied any form of heat.

The sound of a clock striking two came floating in the window when he eventually gave it up and went to bed. Perhaps the morning would produce something that would give him an idea.

It did! But he was quite unprepared for what occurred, and instead of helping to clear up the mystery of Venita Shayne's death it only presented him with a fresh one.

6

The Silent Shot

The first of the swarm of reporters who were to cluster round the house like flies throughout the day arrived just before breakfast. Frank Littlewood was on the staff of the *Echo*, a snub-nosed, cheery young man, whom Lowe knew rather well.

'I was wondering when you'd turn up,' he said, when he interviewed the newcomer at Mr. Hammond's request in the drawing room. 'I can tell you nothing except the bare facts.'

'They'll do to be going on with,' said Littlewood cheerily. 'Is it true, Mr. Lowe, that Venita Shayne's been murdered?' And when the dramatist nodded: 'This is going to cause a sensation, you know that? The most popular actress of the day, the idol of the public, coupled with a murder mystery! What more could any reasonable reporter ask for? How did it happen?'

Lowe supplied him with a brief story. It was useless trying to conceal the facts, and in his opinion it was better that a true account should appear than that it should be left to the imagination of the Press man to conjure up lurid details.

'You've no idea who did it, I suppose?' asked Littlewood, and Lowe shook his head.

'No idea at all!' he answered.

'I'd like to see Hammond. Is he about?'

'There's nobody about except me,' said Lowe. 'And if there were you wouldn't see them. You be satisfied with what you've got, and be thankful for small mercies!'

He got rid of Littlewood just as half a dozen others put in an appearance, and for the next hour he was kept busy. White was having breakfast on the terrace when he joined him, after dealing with the crowd of news-hungry Pressmen.

'It'll keep them quiet for the moment,' said Lowe, as he sat down. 'But they won't go far away, and you can't blame 'em. The fame of the victim and the mysterious circumstances surrounding her murder are enough to excite the whole of Fleet Street. It'll be front-page news for days.'

'We seem to be the only people up,' mumbled the secretary, his mouth full of kidney and bacon.

'Yes. Minter says they're mostly breakfasting in their rooms,' answered the dramatist. 'Personally I'm not sorry.'

'What's the programme for today?' inquired Arnold presently.

Lowe shrugged his shoulders.

'It depends,' he answered. 'I expect Cotter will be back here later. So far as I'm concerned I've no particular programme. I'm just going to be guided by the course of events.'

He had finished his breakfast and just lighted a pipe when Montague Hammond appeared. If he had looked harassed and worried on the previous day he looked positively ghastly this morning. He seemed to have shrunk. His face was pallid and grey, and the skin hung loosely at the corners of his mouth and beneath his eyes.

'Give me some coffee. I want nothing to eat,' he said hoarsely to Minter, and flung himself down in a chair.

As he took the cup, which the butler handed to him Lowe saw that he was shaking as though he had a slight ague.

'I want to talk to you, Hammond,' murmured the dramatist, and the producer shot him a startled glance.

'Talk! Talk!' he said irritably. 'Nothing but talk! That policeman yesterday. Why was this, why was that? Questions and questions! It's driving me frantic!'

'I'm afraid it can't be helped,' said Lowe. 'You must realize Hammond, that every possible source of information must be tapped.'

'I know nothing!' declared the producer. 'I didn't kill Venita. Poor child, I wouldn't have hurt a hair of her head!'

'Nobody imagines for one moment that you did,' said Lowe. 'But you may be in a position to tell us something that would help.'

Hammond looked startled and, Lowe thought, a little frightened.

'What makes you think that?' he

muttered. 'Why d'you think I should know anything?'

'You knew her better than anyone,' answered the dramatist. 'Had she ever mentioned that she was afraid of anybody?'

'Of course not! Is it likely!' Hammond shook his head impatiently. 'Why should Venita be afraid of anybody? She was popular, she was successful. She had no enemies.'

'She must have had one,' said Lowe seriously, and Montague Hammond sprang to his feet.

'Why do you keep reminding me of that?' he cried. 'Why can't you let me forget it? Good God! I can see her now — !'

The man was overwrought. His nerves were strained almost to breaking point.

'Get me some brandy — neat!' he snapped to a passing servant and the girl hurried away.

When she returned with the glass Hammond gulped down the spirit eagerly. Its effect was almost instantly visible. A tinge of colour came into his flabby cheeks and his dull eyes brightened.

'I'm sorry, Lowe,' he apologised. 'But this business has given me an unpleasant shock.'

'It's given us all a shock,' said the dramatist. 'But I can quite realize how it affects you. Come down on the lawn.'

He rose, took his host by the arm, and together they descended the steps of the terrace and strolled towards the river's edge.

'I'm sorry,' began Lowe, after a pause, 'to have to bother you at the present time, but it's essential that everything possible should be done to discover who is responsible for that girl's death without delay. Time is an important factor.'

'I realize that,' muttered Hammond.

'Then tell me,' went on his friend. 'Do you associate that last anonymous letter you received with what happened yesterday?'

He felt Hammond start.

'I — I hadn't thought about it,' he muttered.

Lowe was convinced he was lying. There was no ring of truth his voice.

'I should have thought it would have

been the first thing that occurred to you,' he remarked. 'It was to me.'

'I'd forgotten it,' declared Hammond. 'This other — this horrible thing drove it completely out of my mind. Now I come to think of it there might be something in what you say.'

'There's little doubt that the blonde referred to meant Miss Shayne,' said the dramatist. 'According to the letter she 'was for it', and she got it!'

'What are you suggesting?' whispered Hammond. 'The person who has been sending me these letters and the person who killed Venita is the same?'

'I'm not suggesting anything,' said Lowe gravely. 'I'm asking you to do that. I'm going to be perfectly candid, Hammond. You know more about this than you've said. You've been keeping something back.'

'I? What do you mean?' The producer turned on him angrily, but his eyes failed to meet the other's steady gaze.

'Exactly what I say,' said the dramatist. 'You're keeping something back, Hammond. You know very well why those letters were sent to you, and I think you know why Venita Shayne died!'

Montague Hammond made a gesture as though he was brushing flies from his face.

'I — I don't know anything!' he answered hoarsely. 'God in Heaven, why don't you leave me alone? Haven't I had enough to put up with without these constant and useless questions?'

'Listen to me,' said Lowe. 'Murder is a serious thing. This girl was murdered in your house. She was murdered after you had received a letter hinting at the fate that would overtake her. I don't wish to be hard, Hammond, but in the present circumstances you can hardly expect me to study your feelings at the expense of the truth. Now, what do you know?'

The stout man looked round quickly.

'I — I'll tell you,' he burst out. 'I've been trying to make up my mind to tell you from the first. I do know who wrote those letters, Lowe. It — !' He broke off abruptly, and a thin gasping cry issued from his open mouth.

For a moment he swayed unsteadily,

and then crumpled up to fall twitching at Lowe's feet.

With an exclamation the dramatist knelt beside him. For a moment he thought the stress and strain which Hammond had undergone had brought on a fit of some kind, and then he saw the blood on the big face and the tiny round hole in the right temple from which it trickled.

An expression of incredulous dismay crossed his face. The man had been shot!

There had been no sound, but there was the bullet hole! He ripped open the silk shirt and laid a hand on the broad chest. There was no movement. Montague Hammond was dead; had been killed at the very moment when he had been about to divulge what he knew!

7

The Man on the Island

The shot must have come from the island. Hammond had been standing with his right side to the river frontage when he fell.

Lowe turned and scanned the place keenly, but he could see nothing. It was a strip of land that divided the main stream and was privately owned; a slice of dense shrubbery and woodland that extended for three or four hundred yards.

Arnold White came up at a run, his face anxious.

'What is it?' he asked. 'What's happened to Mr. Hammond?'

'He's been shot!' said Lowe curtly, and the secretary's jaw dropped in his astonishment.

'I heard no report — !' he began.

'There was none,' broke in the dramatist. 'There was nothing but a faint plop, which I thought was made by a bird or a fish in the water. Stay here. I'm going across the river.'

He hurried down to the edge of the lawn and scrambled into one of the punts. Unfastening the painter he paddled the boat swiftly over the placid water and pulled up as the punt's nose bumped gently into the opposite bank. It never crossed his mind that he might be in danger, yet somewhere amongst that dense foliage lurked an armed man who had just committed murder.

He fastened the punt to a thick branch of an overhanging bush and jumped ashore, listening intently. But there was no sound save the twittering of the birds in the trees and the soft lap-lap of the river as it gently washed against the punt.

Lowe stared across towards Backwaters. He could see the motionless figure of Hammond and White standing beside him, but there was no other sign of life visible. The low stone house glistened in the sun, a pleasant and peaceful picture, not at all in keeping with the grim tragedy that had been enacted but a few seconds before.

The island was covered thickly with trees, and dense masses of bramble and rank grass grew almost to the water's edge. He forced his way through this tangle of undergrowth, up the shelving bank, until he came to a spot where walking was easier. Here he stopped again to listen, but nothing greeted his ears. Yet without doubt the shot that had killed Hammond had been fired from somewhere on this piece of land, and not very far away, either.

He began to explore cautiously. The person who had pulled the trigger may have made off after he had seen that his shot had been successful. He began a thorough search, moving slowly and carefully so as not to warn the possible lurker of his approach.

He had covered perhaps a hundred yards when he came to a little clearing, and stopped. Although he had heard nothing, there were visible signs of the presence of someone. A tent was erected beside the thick trunk of an oak, and near it a wisp of smoke indicated the presence of a dying fire. Some empty food tins, a bucket of water, and a frying pan were ranged nearby. He stared at the dark opening of the tent. Was there someone lurking within?

The clearing was surrounded with bushes, and taking advantage of the cover he crept nearer. Presently he was within a few yards of the little shelter, but he could neither hear nor see anyone. Stooping he searched for, and found, a fair sized stone. Taking careful aim he threw it at the bucket and it struck with a clatter. If there was anyone inside, that ought to bring them out, he thought grimly. But it had no effect. The little camp remained deserted. He waited for a second or two and then decided to risk it.

Parting the bushes, keeping a wary and watchful eye on the tent, he covered the short distance that intervened, and looked in. A ground sheet and a few blankets were neatly arranged. A hurricane lamp hung from the centre support, but otherwise the tent was empty.

He frowned. Where was the owner, and what did this temporary habitation signify? Was it the abode of an ordinary summer camper or of someone more sinister? There were notices all round the island forbidding landing. Whoever, therefore, had pitched the tent was either trespassing or had obtained permission from the owner.

Lowe decided to continue his search. Unless the occupant had left by boat from the other side of the island he must be still somewhere about. He moved forward and he was nearing the end of the land when he saw a man coming towards him.

It was a young man with fair hair, dressed in grey flannel trousers and a singlet. He stopped when he saw Lowe, and the two of them stared at each other.

'Is that your camping place up there?' demanded the dramatist.

'What the hell's it got to do with you?' said the stranger.

'You'll find it's got a lot to do with me,' retorted Lowe grimly. 'What are you doing on this island?'

'What are *you* doing?' said the other unpleasantly. 'I don't know who you are, but this is private property and you've no right here at all!'

'Listen,' said the dramatist angrily, 'I

don't want any backchat. A serious crime has just been committed, and I'm looking for the person who did it.'

'A serious crime?' The good-looking face of the man before him changed. 'Why? What's happened?'

'Mr. Hammond, the owner of Backwaters on the mainland, was shot a few minutes ago,' said Lowe. 'And the shot was fired from this island. Now, what do you know about it?'

There was no mistaking the effect of his words. Beneath the sunburn the other's face went pale.

'Hammond shot?' he demanded. 'You're joking!'

'I'm doing nothing of the sort!' retorted Lowe.

'But — but I don't understand.' A bewildered look replaced the one of horrified amazement. 'When did this happen? A few minutes ago, you say? I heard nothing.'

'The shot was fired from either a silenced rifle or an air gun,' said Lowe.

'Good Lord!' Unless he was a very good actor the other was genuinely astonished. 'I suppose you're not trying to put one across me?'

Lowe shook his head.

'I'm serious!' he declared. 'Is there anyone else on this island but you?'

'Not that I'm aware,' was the answer. 'Good Heavens! Hammond!'

'Did you know him?' asked the dramatist quickly.

'Yes, I knew him quite well,' was the reply. 'Look here, tell me more about this business. Who are you and where do you come from?'

'My name is Trevor Lowe,' answered the dramatist, 'and I'm staying at Backwaters, and I don't feel inclined to undergo a cross examination. Do you know anything about the killing of Hammond?'

A flicker of amusement crossed the young man's face.

'If I did I shouldn't be likely to admit it, should I?' he said, and then, suddenly growing serious: 'No, I don't know anything about it. The shot couldn't have come from this island.'

'It couldn't have come from anywhere else,' declared Lowe. 'How long have you been here?'

'Since Friday night,' answered the other hesitantly.

'And you've been all over the island?' inquired the dramatist.

'Most of it,' said the stranger. 'There's nobody else here, I can tell you that. I had to get special permission from old Berryman, who owns the property.'

'That doesn't say somebody didn't row across from the mainland,' said Lowe. 'Have you been down at this end all the morning?'

'Most of it,' admitted the other.

'Then if anyone landed at the other end you wouldn't know anything about it?'

'No, that's true,' agreed the young man. 'Suppose we make a search, shall we?'

'Just a minute,' said Lowe. 'You asked who I am and I told you. Will you return the compliment?'

There was a noticeable reluctance in the stranger's manner.

'I don't see that it matters much, does it?' he said. 'I mean, you can't think I've had any hand in killing old Hammond. Why should I?'

'How can I tell,' retorted the dramatist,

'if I don't know who you are?'

He was pretty sure that the athletic stranger had no knowledge of Hammond's murder. His manner was frank and he hardly looked the type who would have killed secretly.

'Well, look here, I'll tell you who I am,' he said, 'if you won't mention you've seen me to Venita Shayne.'

It was Lowe's turn to be astonished.

'Do you know Venita Shayne?' he asked.

The stranger nodded.

'Yes. But I don't want her to know I'm here. She thinks I'm somewhere else, you see.'

'I should have difficulty in mentioning it to her,' said Lowe slowly. 'She's dead.'

'*What!*' If the news concerning Hammond had startled him, this acted much as the sudden explosion of a bomb a few feet away might have done. 'What d'you mean? How did she die? When — '

'She was murdered yesterday afternoon,' said the dramatist.

'Murdered!' The word came softly, almost inaudibly, and the grey eyes searched Lowe's face. 'You don't mean it?

72

You can't mean it!'

'I'm afraid I do,' he replied.

'Venita!' whispered the young man. 'Dead! It's incredible!'

'Did you know her well?' inquired the dramatist, and the other nodded.

'Yes,' he answered. 'Yes — very — very well.'

'Then I shall have to insist on you telling me who you are,' said Lowe. 'If you knew Miss Shayne the police will want to question you about her and about your presence here.'

'Will it be necessary?' muttered the stranger, and then: 'Yes, I suppose it will. Of course it will. Oh well, I'll tell you. My name is Cavendish. Harold Cavendish!'

8

The Letter

Lowe surveyed the well-knit figure of the man before him and nothing of the astonishment he felt appeared in his face. So this was the Honourable Harold Cavendish, son of Lord Glenriven, to whom Venita Shayne, at that last dinner, had announced she was engaged.

It was queer, he thought, that there was nothing of grief in the other's expression. Surprise, yes. Horror, a little, but no sign of sorrow. Rather did he detect a faint trace of relief.

'You were engaged to her, weren't you?' he said, breaking the awkward silence.

'Who told you that?' demanded Cavendish swiftly.

'Miss Shayne,' said the dramatist. 'She told all of us last night at dinner.'

Cavendish frowned.

'She — she shouldn't have done that,'

he muttered. 'She promised to keep it secret.' He was apparently a little perturbed that the engagement had been made known.

'What are you doing here, Mr. Cavendish?' asked Lowe curiously. 'It appears to me rather peculiar that you should be camping out on this island so near to the house in which Miss Shayne was spending the weekend.'

'I suppose it does,' said Cavendish. 'But I don't propose to enlighten you concerning my reasons.'

'The police will wish to know,' said Lowe swiftly.

'It's no concern of anybody's,' declared the young man. 'If I like to come down for the weekend that's my affair, isn't it?'

'Under ordinary circumstances, yes,' answered Lowe a little impatiently. 'But you must realise, Mr. Cavendish, that these are no ordinary circumstances. Two people have been murdered, two people who were known to you.'

'I've already told you that I had nothing to do with Hammond's death,' said the other, 'and the same applies to Venita.'

'But you were in the vicinity,' said the dramatist, 'under rather curious circumstances, and you'll have to explain.'

Cavendish's jaw set stubbornly.

'It's nobody's business but my own!' he declared. 'I came here for certain reasons which concern me, and only me.'

'To be near Miss Shayne?' hazarded Lowe, and saw that his guess had been right.

'Well, yes, if you like,' said Cavendish. 'It's not extraordinary, is it? We were engaged.'

'You could have come to the house. Why the secrecy?' demanded the dramatist.

'I'm not answering any more questions,' said the young man stiffly, and Lowe shrugged his shoulders.

'Very well. If you like to adopt that attitude,' he said, 'you must take the consequences.'

He did not believe that the man before him had had any hand in either of the two murders, but he was curious to know why Cavendish should have chosen to camp on that island. What had brought him to the vicinity of Backwaters during that weekend? Was it just to be near Venita Shayne, or was it — an idea occurred to him — was it to spy on the girl? Was it jealousy? That didn't coincide with the subtle expression of relief that he had detected when Cavendish had learned that Venita was dead. There was nothing of the ardent lover about him.

He kept his thoughts to himself, however, and suggested that they could make a search of the island to see if any traces could be found of someone else's presence.

Cavendish readily agreed, and they made a thorough survey, but without result. The only boats were the covered punt in which Cavendish had come himself, and the one belonging to Backwaters. Neither was there any sign of anybody else having been there. There had been ample time, of course, while Lowe was talking to Cavendish for the murderer to have escaped. It would take barely three minutes to row across to the mainland, very little more to have swum the distance. Neither could they be sure that there wasn't someone still concealed on the island. The undergrowth was thick; the trees were like a forest. It would not be impossible for a man to remain hidden. It was useless, however, to continue the search, and Lowe decided to give it up.

'I'm afraid I shall have to ask you to accompany me to Backwaters,' he said, and this apparently did not at all meet with Mr. Cavendish's approval.

'Why?' he demanded.

'Surely the reason is obvious,' answered the dramatist. 'I can't leave you here. The police will undoubtedly want to question you, and if you decided to clear off it might lead to a lot of unpleasantness.'

They argued for some time, and eventually the young man grudgingly consented.

'Wait while I put on a shirt,' he said, and went into his tent. He emerged in a little while in an open-neck silk shirt and joined Lowe, who had waited outside.

'Now I'm ready,' he remarked, and the dramatist made his way back to the punt.

White was still waiting by the body of

Hammond, and as Lowe brought the boat up to the landing stage and stepped ashore he came down to the water's edge.

'I've notified Minter,' he said, 'and he's breaking the news to Mrs. Hammond.' He stared at Cavendish curiously.

'This is Mr. Cavendish,' said his employer. 'He was engaged to Miss Shayne.' And White's astonishment was more obvious than polite. 'You'd better get on the telephone,' went on the dramatist, 'and notify Inspector Cotter of this second crime.'

The secretary nodded and hurried way, and Cavendish stared rather fearfully at the dead producer.

'Poor old Hammond,' he murmured.

'How well did you know him?' asked Lowe.

'Not very well,' said the young man. 'I met him at parties and of course at first nights. He was a cheery chap. In fact he introduced me to Venita.' His face clouded as the name passed his lips. 'How — how was she killed?' he asked. 'The same way?'

Lowe shook his head.

'No. She was strangled,' he replied.

'Good God! How awful!' whispered Cavendish, and he looked genuinely horrified. 'Have — have you any idea who could have done it?'

'Not the slightest,' said the dramatist. 'Though I've no doubt it won't be long before the police find out.'

Minter came hurriedly down the steps of the terrace and approached him.

'Will you go to the mistress, Mr. Lowe,' said the man shakily. Evidently the shock of his master's death had been a severe one. 'She wants to see you — urgently.'

Lowe nodded.

'I'll go at once,' he said. 'This is Mr. Cavendish, Minter. Look after him, will you?'

He hurried into the house, coming face to face with Marjorie Lovelace as he entered the lounge.

'Is it true?' whispered the girl. 'Has Monty been — killed?'

'Yes,' he said gravely. 'I should advise you to stay indoors, Miss Lovelace, until after the police have been. I'm going to see Mrs. Hammond.'

He found a frightened maid in the hall and she directed him to his hostess's bedroom. It was on the first floor, and tapping on the door he waited. A thin, husky voice bade him 'come in,' and turning the handle he entered.

It was a large, airy room over the lounge. The windows faced the river, and in a silk-draped bed lay Mrs. Hammond. Her thin face was ghastly; and the shadows under her eyes were so pronounced that they looked like caverns.

'So my husband is dead,' she said, fixing her eyes on him in an unwavering and rather disconcerting stare.

He nodded in silence, he could think of nothing to say.

'Minter tells me he was shot,' she went on. 'Is that true?'

'I'm afraid it is,' he murmured sympathetically.

'The Shayne girl was strangled,' said Mrs. Hammond. 'It was a bad day for Monty when he took up with her.'

'Are you suggesting,' said the dramatist, 'that Miss Shayne was indirectly responsible for what happened to your husband?'

'Of course,' said the woman. 'She was killed, too, wasn't she? The same person killed both of them.'

'Do you know that?' he asked quickly.

'No. I don't *know* it, but I feel it here.' She tapped her thin breast. 'I'm sure of it! If Monty had never met Venita Shayne he'd be alive today. Did he tell you why he was afraid of her?'

He was startled, the question came so suddenly and so abruptly. 'I wasn't aware he was afraid of her,' he said.

'Then he *didn't* tell you.' The woman nodded quickly with little bird-like jerks of the head. 'He didn't tell you. But he *was*. He was afraid of Venita Shayne. She made him do anything she wanted. Was it she who wrote those letters?'

Again he was startled.

'You mean the anonymous letters?' he said.

'Of course I mean them! He told you about them, didn't he? Isn't that why you're down here?'

'Yes. But what makes you think Miss Shayne wrote them?' he inquired.

'I didn't say I did think she wrote

them,' answered Mrs. Hammond. 'I merely said did she? It wouldn't surprise me. Nothing about Venita Shayne would ever surprise me. You thought she was sweet and beautiful and everything that was lovely, didn't you? Oh, go on! You might as well admit it,' she said impatiently as he hesitated. 'Every man thought that about her, but she wasn't. She was a callous, calculating little devil! A cruel little devil! I'm glad she's dead!'

'Mrs. Hammond!' he protested, genuinely shocked.

'Why shouldn't I say what I mean?' she asked. 'Why should I be hypocritical and pretend to feel sorry when I'm not. I'm glad she's dead, d'you hear!' She raised herself off the pillows on to one elbow. 'I asked you to come and see me,' she continued rapidly, and her excitement had brought a spot of red into her cheeks, 'because I want you to find out who killed Monty. Find out who killed him. Find out what was behind the killing of Venita Shayne. You'll stir up a lot of mud and it won't be pleasant, but find out!'

Before he could open his lips to reply

there came a tap on the door.

'Come in,' said Mrs. Hammond breath-lessly, sinking back on pillows, and her maid entered.

She carried a letter on a salver, which she held out to Lowe.

'For me?' he said in surprise.

The girl nodded.

'Yes, sir. I've just found it in the box,' she answered.

He took the envelope, saw the illiterate scrawl, and his eyes narrowed. With a swift movement and a murmured apology he put his thumb under the flap and ripped it open.

The envelope contained a single sheet of paper on which had been roughly printed, by the same hand as the superscription, the following message:

'The blonde's gone, and when you get this Hammond will have gone, too. A nice pair. There's more to follow, so watch out.'

In place of the signature was the scrawled drawing of the dangling man.

9

Cotter's Theory

'Well, Mr. Lowe,' said Inspector Cotter, fixing his shrewd brown eyes on the dramatist and gently pulling at the lobe of his right ear. 'What do you make of it, eh?'

He had arrived almost on the heels of the anonymous letter, and listened with interest to the story of the second murder.

'I should like to postpone answering that question,' said Lowe. 'It's a little early yet to think anything.'

'In my opinion,' said the inspector, 'there's not much doubt. It was a bit of a puzzler, I'll admit, before, but this second crime has straightened things out.'

'Oh, you think so?' murmured Lowe.

Cotter nodded.

'Yes, sir, I most certainly do!' he replied. 'To my mind the presence of this man Cavendish on the island clears everything up.'

'Meaning that you're under the impression that Cavendish is the murderer,' said the dramatist.

Again Cotter nodded.

'Yes,' he answered. 'And I don't think I'm far wrong either. His manner's queer, and he won't answer questions. His explanation as to why he was on the island is a bit thin, you must admit.'

'It's rather extraordinary, Inspector,' said Lowe, 'how thin the truth sometimes sounds.'

'Yes, I'll admit that, sir,' agreed Cotter. 'But in this case — ' He shook his head. 'No, I don't think we've got to look any further than Cavendish.'

'What's your idea regarding the motive, then?' asked the dramatist.

'It's evident, sir,' replied Cotter. 'I've been making one or two inquiries in the village, and it was pretty general knowledge that this girl Shayne and Hammond were — well, pretty thick. In my opinion jealousy was at the bottom of it. This fellow Cavendish found out and killed 'em both.'

'But how?' murmured Lowe. 'How did

he kill Miss Shayne?'

An expression of complacency came into the thin face of the man before him.

'I've worked that out,' he said. 'The household were on the lawn, weren't they? And the servant Minter was in the hall. Miss Shayne was up here writing letters,' — he waved his hand round the study in which they were seated. 'Well, Cavendish swam across! There's a herbaceous border running right down to the water's edge, backed by arches of climbing roses, and behind it a little path that leads up to the house. You've noticed that?'

Lowe nodded.

'Well,' went on Cotter, 'this fellow Cavendish, as I said, swims across. He lands by the little path and he crawls out of the water. The people on the lawn wouldn't see him because he'd be screened by the roses. He creeps up the little path towards the house, and he finds a window open. He enters, makes his way up to the study, kills the girl, and departs by the way he came.'

'Surely he'd have left some traces?' said

the dramatist. 'He would have been wet, for instance.'

'No, sir.' Cotter shook his head. 'It was a very hot afternoon. It wouldn't have taken him two or three minutes to become bone dry.'

Lowe pursed his lips. The theory was possible, he had to admit that, and it had not occurred to him. It was quite conceivable that the murderer could have come from the riverside and gained access to the house as the inspector had suggested. The difficulty lay in how he had reached the study. He mentioned this.

'It might have been difficult, but it's not impossible,' said Cotter. 'Minter was in the hall, I know, but it would have been fairly easy for this fellow, once he was in the house, to wait until the servants' attention was distracted and then slip up the stairs.'

'He would be taking an appalling risk,' said Lowe, but Cotter disagreed.

'Scarcely any risk at all, sir,' he declared. 'Just you think for a moment. He was engaged to Miss Shayne and was known to Hammond. If he'd been spotted by Minter he had an excuse. He'd been camping on the island and he'd swum across to see his fiancée. If he'd been seen there'd have been no murder, but when he found he *hadn't* been seen he carried out his original intentions. I'm sure I'm right! It accounts for everything. Naturally Miss Shayne wouldn't have been suspicious. *He* could easily have got hold of that statuette and come up behind her. And no stranger could, that's definite!'

'Yes, that's definite,' agreed Lowe. 'The person who killed Venita Shayne was known to her.'

'And it was Cavendish!' said Cotter stubbornly. 'If I was a betting man I'd bet anything on it!'

'Well, I'm not sure that you're right,' said the dramatist. 'Mind you,' he added quickly, 'I'm not suggesting that you're wrong. I'm maintaining an open mind.'

'Well, we shall see, sir,' said the inspector. 'Anyway, that's my general theory and that's the line I'm going to work on. There's one thing I'm rather curious to know, and that's what you were doing here, sir? Were you just on a friendly visit — ' he stopped. 'Or weren't you?' he ended lamely.

'Well, not altogether,' said Lowe slowly, 'and I think, Inspector, when I tell you exactly why I was here you'll have to reconsider your theory.'

Briefly he gave an account of the anonymous letters which Hammond had received, and the mysterious watcher whom he had seen on various occasions, ending by handing the inspector the latest one, which had arrived that morning.

Cotter examined it and scratched his chin.

'It's all very peculiar,' he admitted, 'but I don't see any necessity for me to alter my original idea. Why couldn't Cavendish have sent those letters to try and scare Hammond?'

'At the time they started he and Miss Shayne were not engaged,' Lowe pointed out. 'Besides which these letters are just the usual type. They don't accuse Hammond of anything, they're merely abusive and threatening. The only thing queer about them is that little drawing in place of a signature.'

'Cavendish may not have been engaged to the girl,' said the inspector, 'but he must have known her for some time. A fellow hasn't got to be engaged to be jealous. But it seems to me to be common property that she and Hammond were as thick as thieves.'

'Well, I still prefer to keep an open mind on the matter,' declared Trevor Lowe. 'What are you proposing to do, arrest Cavendish?'

Cotter shook his head.

'No, sir,' he answered. 'I haven't sufficient evidence at the moment. I'm detainin' everybody until after the inquest, Cavendish amongst them. And I shall put a man on to watch him so that he can't make a bolt for it.'

'I think you're wise,' agreed the dramatist. 'Wise in not arresting him, I mean. It's my belief we may learn a great deal if we go farther into the history of Venita Shayne.'

'I'm attending to that, sir,' said the inspector. 'She had a flat in Weymouth Street and I've arranged with the police to take possession of it. I'm going up this afternoon as a matter of fact. I've also got the address of her bankers and her lawyers from that fellow Norman who acted as her press agent.'

'Any objection if I come with you?' asked Lowe.

'No, sir,' answered the inspector. 'I shall be very pleased.'

'Then if you like,' said the dramatist, 'I'll drive you up. There'll be a post mortem on Hammond, of course?'

Cotter nodded.

'I think the bullet is likely to be interesting,' Lowe went on. 'I'm under the impression it was fired from an air gun. The faint sound I heard wasn't loud enough for a silenced rifle.'

'He died instantly,' said the inspector, 'according to the doctor. The bullet lodged in the brain. I'm going to have a look through the effects. I've got all his keys.' He rose. 'Perhaps you'd care to give me a hand?'

Lowe agreed and they began at the desk. Methodically and carefully they went through every drawer, examining the papers and documents which each contained and replacing them. There wasn't anything of great interest, and nothing at all that threw any light on the murders.

The desk mostly contained receipts and bills concerning Backwaters and several letters dealing with Mr. Hammond's theatrical interests. There was a cheque book, which a glance showed to concern a private account of Hammond's with a bank in Bray. The cheques were mostly drawn to self and various items connected with household expenses. There was one for a hundred and fifty pounds, the destination of which, however, was not noted on the counterfoil.

'It'll be worthwhile to check that up,' said Lowe, and Cotter agreed.

'You thinking of blackmail?' he remarked.

'No, I'm not, Inspector,' answered Lowe with a smile. 'I'm not thinking of anything. But every other cheque has been meticulously entered on the counterfoil and this one hasn't, therefore it's worth looking into.'

Having exhausted the desk they turned

their attention to the safe. This contained several account books, a sum of money in a cashbook, which amounted to seventy-five pounds, and bundles of old cheque counterfoils and old cheques. These were arranged in piles and neatly encircled with rubber bands. There was a folder bearing the name of the Bray bank, containing passbook sheets. These Cotter placed on one side to be gone through at a later period.

It was right at the back of the safe, and underneath all the other contents, that they came upon a long envelope, heavily sealed. It bore no superscription, and after a moment's hesitation they opened it.

It contained a marriage certificate. The ink was faded, the paper yellowish with age. Lowe looked at the date. It was April 8th 1911 — twenty-six years ago. It certified the marriage of Molly Dwyer, whose occupation was described as 'parlour maid', to James Hinkley, actor.

Why had Hammond preserved the document? The marriage had been celebrated at the Bloomsbury Registrar's office, and Hammond's name did not figure, even as a witness.

'Queer,' muttered Cotter. 'Perhaps his wife could tell us.'

But Mrs. Hammond could tell them nothing. She had never heard of either of the people mentioned, and was not aware that the certificate had been in her husband's possession.

'Oh, well,' said the inspector, 'I don't suppose it's got anything to do with this business.'

But here he was wrong. That twenty-six-year-old marriage certificate was, had he but known it, the reason why two people had already suffered violent deaths, and why a third was to follow before many days had passed.

10

The Maid's Story

Venita Shayne's flat in Weymouth Street was on the third floor of one of those ugly modern buildings that resemble factories more than anything else. A huge block, pierced by many windows and without the slightest pretensions to beauty of any kind. It was a place of thick carpets and polished doors, concealed lighting and porters in sombre uniforms. Very expensive, very up-to-date, and very uncomfortable.

A lift took Trevor Lowe and Inspector Cotter up to the dead woman's flat, and they were admitted by a hard-faced servant. A sergeant of police was sitting in the hall, perched rather uncomfortably on a fragile-looking chair. He had been sent round at Inspector Cotter's request to take charge of the premises, and looked rather relieved that the inspector had arrived.

'Saucy bit of goods,' he confided, jerking his head towards the door through which the maid had vanished after letting them in. 'Wouldn't admit me at first.'

'Thought she looked rather disagreeable,' said Cotter. 'Never mind, Sergeant. We'll take over now.' He called the woman, and she came sullenly. 'What's your name?' he asked.

'Elizabeth Stokes,' she answered shortly.

'How long have you been in the employ of Miss Shayne?' went on the inspector.

'Two years,' said the woman. She was abrupt to the verge of rudeness, and there was no sign of grief in her appearance.

'You've heard, of course, that she has been murdered,' said Cotter, and she nodded.

'Yes. *He* told me,' she said, and made a gesture towards the sergeant.

'What sort of a mistress was Miss Shayne?' asked Trevor Lowe quietly.

'Bad tempered and very difficult to please!' said the maid. 'She looked like an angel and behaved like a devil!'

'How d'you mean?' said Cotter quickly.

'She was always finding fault,' said the

woman. 'Nothing was ever right. And her temper — when she got in one of her rages her language was dreadful.'

'And yet you stayed with her for two years,' murmured the dramatist.

'Well, I've got to earn my living, haven't I?' flashed the woman angrily. 'And she paid well, I will say that.'

'Did she have many visitors?' asked the inspector.

'No, not many,' replied the maid. 'She used to give cocktail parties now and again, but she hadn't many friends — not as far as I know. And I'm not surprised.'

'Why?' It was Lowe who put the question.

'She was so uppish and conceited!' explained the woman. 'There wasn't anybody else on the earth so far as she was concerned, except Venita Shayne. I suppose it was natural, spoilt as she was.'

'Who were the people who used to visit her?' said Cotter. 'Do you remember their names?'

'Some of them.' She wrinkled her forehead. 'There was Mr. Hammond. He was a pretty regular visitor. And then there was Mr. Cavendish. He came several times, mostly to tea. And there was a little feller, queer little man, like a bank clerk. He used to come at all odd times. I don't know his name. Miss Shayne used to call him Joe. And — ' she stopped.

'Go on, and what?' said Cotter sharply.

'There was somebody here last night,' she continued, 'and I don't know who it was, neither. I only caught a glimpse of him.'

'What d'you mean?' said Lowe. 'Somebody called here last night?'

'They didn't exactly call,' said the woman. 'I'll tell you. I'd gone to bed early, I wasn't feeling too good, and with her away there was a chance of having a rest. You didn't get much when she was about. I'd fallen asleep when I heard a sound that woke me. It was the faint rattle of a bolt being drawn and it came from here. My room's along there at the back. I thought at first she'd come back, and I got out of bed and opened my bedroom door. The place was in darkness, but a light burns all night on the landing outside, and sufficient comes in through the fanlight to show up the hall dimly. There was someone fumbling at the front door and I called out. Then the door was opened and I just caught a glimpse of a man as he slipped through and shut it after him.'

'Isn't there a night porter?' asked Cotter.

'Yes,' said the woman.

'Did you notify him?'

She shook her head.

'Not me. For all I know it might have been Mr. Hammond,' she said. 'He's got a key.'

'Oh, he had a key, did he?' said Lowe. 'But how could it have been Mr. Hammond? You said this man pulled back the bolt?'

A puzzled expression came into the servant's face. 'I never thought of that,' she admitted. 'Of course, being on my own I'd bolted the door, which I don't usually do. He couldn't have got in that way, could he?'

'Why didn't you tell me about this, Miss?' put in the sergeant.

'Haven't I said,' she snapped, 'that I thought it might have been Mr. Hammond? I thought perhaps he'd been up in town late and Miss Shayne had asked him to fetch something. I didn't want to advertise the fact that he'd got a key. I might have got into trouble for not minding me own business.'

'Did the man's appearance suggest Mr. Hammond to you?' said the inspector.

'His appearance didn't suggest nothing to me,' answered the woman. 'I only caught sight of him for a moment, and then he had gone.'

'The question is, how did he get in?' murmured the dramatist. 'Is there a fire-escape?'

She nodded.

'Yes. An iron staircase affair passes by a door in the kitchen.'

'Is that kept locked?' said the inspector.

'Always!' she answered.

'Show us,' ordered Lowe. 'I'm rather interested in this midnight visitor.'

She led the way through to a spotless kitchen and pointed to a small door by the side of the window. The dramatist tried it. It was locked.

'Where do you keep the key?' he asked.

She pointed to the white enamel dresser.

'There,' she said, and then with a sharp intake of her breath: 'Why, it's gone!' She went quickly over and peered along the shelf, but there was no sign of a key. 'It's gone!' she repeated. 'Now who could have took it?'

'When did you last see it?' asked Lowe.

She puckered up her brows in thought.

'Friday,' she answered after a pause. 'I was cleaning the dresser down, and I remember putting it back.'

'Well, there's no question how the man got in, whoever he was,' remarked Lowe. 'He came up the fire-escape, opened the door with the key, and relocked it behind him.'

'And took the key away with him,' supplemented Inspector Cotter. 'Now what did he come for? Did Miss Shayne keep any money or jewellery here?'

'No,' said the woman. 'She seldom carried much money, she didn't need to. When she went out other people mostly paid. The greater part of her jewellery she kept at her bank. What she was wearing she took with her, of course.'

'So there's nothing of value to tempt a burglar — ' began the inspector, and Lowe interrupted him.

'I shouldn't waste your time over the burglar theory,' he said. 'At least, not an ordinary burglar. How could this man have got hold of the key?' He addressed the last part of his remark to the woman.

'I don't know,' she said.

'There have been no strangers in the flat since last Friday — since you last saw it?'

'No.'

'Perhaps Miss Shayne took it away with her?' suggested Cotter and Elizabeth Stokes agreed that this was possible.

She had seen it last on the Friday but couldn't remember whether it had been there or not after Venita Shayne had left to go down to Backwaters.

'She arrived with a Mr. Norman,' said Lowe. 'Did he call for her?'

'Yes,' said the servant. 'He was one of 'em that was often here.'

'You didn't say so,' said Inspector Cotter. 'When I asked for names of the people who called frequently you didn't mention Mr. Norman.'

'I'd forgotten,' said the woman.

'Well, the person who used the key came for something,' muttered the dramatist. 'The thing is, did he get it or didn't he? I suppose you could tell if there was anything missing?'

'I dunno that I could,' said the maid. 'Miss Shayne had a lot of things which she kept locked up.'

'We'd better make a search,' said Lowe. 'We came to do that, anyhow.'

Cotter agreed.

The flat was a large one. There were three bedrooms and two reception rooms, apart from the kitchen, bathroom, and a tiny cupboard-like apartment that was used for the storage of trunks and oddments. The bigger of the three bedrooms had been used by the dead girl. It was here they began their search.

Cotter had provided himself with a bunch of keys, and with these he unlocked the drawers of the dressing table. There were the usual articles of make-up, etc., but nothing of interest. The wardrobe was full of clothing and a dressing-chest contained an enormous variety of flimsy underwear, nightdresses, stockings and similar articles of feminine apparel.

'There's nothing here,' he said, and they turned their attention to the lounge.

There was a desk in one corner and this contained an assortment of paid and unpaid bills, letters and photographs. There were dozens of photographs, Venita Shayne in every conceivable pose and costume. The drawer was full of them. The letters proved to be of little account. They were mostly invitations to parties from various friends.

The maid, who had followed them curiously during their search, came forward as they finished with the desk.

'She had her diary with her, I suppose,' she remarked, and Lowe, who had gone over to a low bookcase, swung round sharply.

'Diary?' he said. 'Did she keep a diary?'

'Oh yes, she kept a diary,' said

Elizabeth Stokes. 'A thick, leather-bound book with a lock and key. It used to lie on her desk there.'

'Did you find any diary amongst her luggage at Backwaters?' said the dramatist to Cotter, and he shook his head.

'No, sir. There was no diary there.' His shrewd eyes looked at the other with an unspoken question.

The dramatist nodded.

'Yes, I think so,' he said softly. 'That's what the man in the night came for; Venita Shayne's diary!'

11

A Surprising Statement

They completed their search of the flat, but the missing diary did not come to light. Either Venita Shayne had put it somewhere in safe keeping before leaving to spend the weekend at Backwaters, or the night intruder had taken it away with him.

'Can you remember seeing this diary after Miss Shayne had left?' Lowe asked the maid.

'I didn't come into this room till now,' she answered, and he raised his eyebrows.

'Surely when you were dusting — ' he began.

'I didn't do any dusting,' she broke in. 'I was going to give the place a clean-up on Monday before she came back. I get little enough rest and when I do get a chance — '

'Oh, yes, I understand,' said the

dramatist hastily. He had no wish to listen to a long discourse upon the woman's grievances. 'Well, I don't think we can do much more here, Cotter. We may as well be getting back.'

The inspector was in agreement. Except for what they had learned concerning the missing diary they had discovered nothing of any value. Venita Shayne seemed to have started life when, under the auspices of Mr. Hammond, she had suddenly leaped to fame. There was not the faintest indication of her previous existence among the contents of the flat. No old letters, papers, or anything that dated earlier than three years previously.

It would not be difficult to trace up her previous history. She had been a provincial actress when Hammond had found her, and therefore several people would be in a position to give an account of her earlier life. But it was strange that she had kept no memento of these days, no photographs or old playbills or programmes, or anything that related to that period of her life before she had become famous. There may have been some reference in the missing diary — Lowe thought very possibly there was — but before they could be sure it had to be found, and that appeared likely to be difficult.

They left the flat at six o'clock, after locking and sealing all the rooms with the exception of the kitchen and Elizabeth Stokes' bedroom, and started on the return journey to Backwaters.

There were no other inquiries to be pursued in Town for it was Sunday, and in that abnormal heat it was unlikely they would find the people they wished to see at home.

'Well, Cotter,' said Lowe, as they sped along. 'How does this new development fit in with your theory?'

'It fits in very well, Mr. Lowe,' said the inspector. 'It's my belief that it was Cavendish who took that diary.'

'You're not going to let Cavendish go without a struggle, I can see that,' murmured the dramatist, with a faint smile.

'No, sir, I'm not!' declared the inspector. 'Because I believe he's the fellow we want.'

'And what makes you think he should take all the trouble to come to London to steal the dead woman's diary?' asked Lowe.

'Because he hoped to find something in it,' answered Cotter swiftly, 'that would clinch his suspicion. And I believe he did. That's why he shot Hammond.'

'I see. You're still convinced then that jealousy is the motive for these two murders?'

'I am!' asserted the inspector. 'And you'll find I'm right, Mr. Lowe.'

'Surely,' said the dramatist, 'if he wasn't sure that his suspicions were correct, he wouldn't have killed the girl first and gone to collect the evidence after.'

'I'm not so certain of that.' Cotter was evidently not going to have his original idea shaken. 'She may have said something, taunted him with the diary — anything. You know how these things are, Mr. Lowe. Whatever happened, I believe that's the solution.'

'Well, we shall see,' remarked the dramatist. 'I'm under the impression that there's something very much more serious behind this business.'

He relapsed into silence, occupying the rest of the journey by reviewing the case in his mind. And he found it a queer and a fascinating problem.

What had Hammond been about to disclose when the shot had silenced him? He had known something, something that had frightened him, something that was connected with those anonymous letters — and the watcher who had dogged his footsteps. Something that also connected these incidents with the death of Venita Shayne. Was there any truth in the rumour that there had been something more than friendship between the producer and the dead woman, or was this just the usual malicious gossip? It was obvious that Mrs. Hammond believed it. A callous, calculating little devil, she had called the girl. And Elizabeth Stokes had also declared that her mistress had been difficult, and bad-tempered.

At the police station he dropped the inspector and drove thoughtfully alone to Backwaters. Arnold White met him in the drive, a rather harassed look on his face.

'I'm glad you've got back,' he said with

relief. 'The reporters have been swarming round this place all day like bees.'

'I guessed they would,' said the dramatist, as he slipped from behind the wheel and stretched himself. 'Any other news?'

The secretary shook his head.

'No, except that confinement to the house seems to be playing the deuce with everyone's nerves,' he answered.

'That's only to be expected,' said his employer. 'You can't drop murder into the middle of a house party and expect everyone to go on behaving normally. Where's Cavendish?'

'Sitting on the lawn talking to Eric Norman,' said Arnold. 'Mrs. Hammond hasn't appeared all day. Miss Lovelace and John Moore went on the river for a bit this afternoon, and now they've gone for a walk. Dinner 'ull be ready in about twenty minutes.'

'All right, put the car away,' said the dramatist, 'and then come up to my room. I'm going to have a wash.'

He was laving his face when Arnold joined him.

'Nobody's dressing, I suppose?' he

said, and the secretary shook his head.

'No,' he answered. 'Mrs. Hammond sent word that there was no necessity. How did you know?'

'Well, you're not dressed,' mumbled Lowe from the depths of a towel, 'and I caught a glimpse of Norman and he's still talking to Cavendish. I hardly suppose Miss Lovelace and John Moore are strolling about in evening clothes, and they won't have time to change. Not very difficult is it?'

White grinned.

'No, I suppose it isn't,' he confessed. 'How did you get on in Town?'

Lowe told him, and the secretary screwed up his face.

'Queer about that diary,' he commented. 'Must have been important or the fellow wouldn't have taken the risk. How d'you think he got the key?'

'I don't know. It's been puzzling me.' Lowe was changing his clothes as he spoke. 'According to the maid no strangers entered the flat between the time she last saw it and the time we made the discovery it was gone.'

'Which looks as if Miss Shayne must have taken it herself,' said White.

'That's possible,' agreed the dramatist.

'In which case the man who killed her stole it out of her handbag,' continued the secretary. 'That seems plausible enough to me.'

'It's plausible enough,' agreed his employer. 'But why did he take it? Why did he want that diary?'

'Why did he kill Venita Shayne?' retorted White. 'Have you got any theory?'

Lowe shook his head.

'Not at present,' he answered. 'But Cotter has. And he's not only got a theory but he's convinced it's the true one.'

He gave a brief outline of the inspector's idea, and Arnold pursed his lips.

'I've been talking a lot to Cavendish during the day,' he said, 'and he doesn't give me the impression of being a murderer.'

'If one could discover murderers by talking to them,' said Lowe, 'police work would become a sinecure.'

'Yes, but Cavendish isn't the right type for this sort of crime,' said White stubbornly. 'I can imagine him pulling a gun and shooting in a temper, but I can't imagine him strangling a woman.'

'Neither can I,' agreed Lowe. 'I think your psychology is sound.'

The silver tinkle of a gong warned them that dinner was ready, and they went downstairs. The meal was a gloomy one. The vacant places brought back to everyone the shadow that hung over the house. Eric Norman ate scarcely anything, and Cavendish was obviously ill at ease. Lowe tried valiantly more than once to start a topic of conversation, but he only received monosyllabic replies, and eventually gave it up. Marjorie Lovelace looked pale and tired. John Moore, although he made a good meal, scarcely raised his eyes once from the plate before him.

The evening was sultry and hot as might be expected after the unusual heat of the day, and coffee was served on the loggia. The girl excused herself immediately after on the plea of a headache, and went to her room. John Moore, after a few desultory remarks, took Lowe to one side and inquired how long he thought they would all be detained.

'Certainly until after the inquest,' said the dramatist, and the young actor moved gloomily away.

Cavendish walked down to the river edge and stood staring at the glass-like surface of the water, leaving Eric Norman, White and Lowe alone.

'I've been waiting for the opportunity of a word with you, Lowe,' said the press agent, after a quick glance round. 'How are things going?'

'If you mean,' said the dramatist, 'have we made any startling discovery, no!'

'It's a shocking affair altogether,' said Norman in a low voice. 'Poor Venita's death was terrible enough, but Hammond's coming on top of it — who d'you think's responsible?'

'I haven't the least idea,' said Lowe, and then: 'You knew Venita Shayne as well as anyone, Norman. What sort of a girl was she?'

'How d'you mean?' said the other quickly.

'Well, I mean what sort of disposition

116

had she?' explained the dramatist. 'Was she the sort of girl who made enemies easily?'

'Good Lord, no!' Norman's tone was emphatic. 'Venita was the sweetest kid that was ever born. Why did you ask that?' He eyed the other curiously.

'I was just wondering,' answered Lowe vaguely. 'There must be some reason for her death, Norman, you know. She was hated by someone. Hated so much that whoever hated her went to the length of murder to appease this hatred.'

'Yes. It's unbelievable.' Norman crushed out his cigarette in his coffee saucer, although it was barely half smoked. 'Unbelievable! I can't understand what reason anyone could have had for harming Venita.'

'How long had you known her?' asked Lowe.

'Let me see.' The press agent took out another cigarette with nervous fingers. 'Nearly three years. Ever since she first became famous. Hammond introduced us and asked me to boost her. Poor old Hammond. He thought a lot of Venita; too much, I've suspected more than once.'

'So you hinted the other day,' said Lowe.

'Oh, I don't think there was anything — ' Norman paused searching for words — 'well, you know what I mean. People talk, of course. In the theatrical profession they slander one another very fluently, particularly someone who's successful. But I think he had a soft spot for her all the same. It gave him a shock when she sprang that engagement on us.'

'It gave you one, too,' said Lowe quietly, and Norman nodded.

'Yes, it did,' he answered. 'I'm willing to admit it. I was a little hurt, too, that she hadn't told me before. I've been talking to Cavendish. It's queer, he doesn't seem nearly so cut up as I should have expected.'

This had been Lowe's view, too, but he said nothing.

'What was he doing on that island?' went on Norman. 'Peculiar idea, don't you think, coming down to camp out with Venita staying almost opposite? I mean, it's so unnecessary. Hammond would have invited him here like a shot if she had suggested it.'

'According to what he says,' replied Lowe, 'he didn't want her to know he was here. She thought he was somewhere else altogether. As you say, it's peculiar. But then the whole thing's peculiar.'

'You're right there,' agreed Norman. 'Reverting to Cavendish. To judge by his manner you'd think he was glad that Venita been killed.'

'Perhaps he's one of those people who object to showing their emotions,' said Lowe, 'and the result of trying to hide his sorrow gives you that impression.'

'That may be it,' said the press agent. 'But all the same — ' he stopped as Lowe gave him a warning glance, for the subject of their conversation was strolling towards them.

'It looks as though we're in for a storm.' The voice of Cavendish floated quietly through the gathering gloom. 'It's pretty black over there.'

Lowe murmured a conventional reply as the young man joined them and dropped into a chair by his side. The conversation became fragmentary and desultory, and after a little while Eric Norman rose with a yawn and announced his intention of going to bed.

As he entered the house Lowe gave White a warning kick, and taking the rather pronounced hint he, too, got up, said 'good night' and followed in the wake of the press agent.

After they had gone there was a short silence, broken at last by Lowe.

'I'm under the impression, Mr. Cavendish, that you want to tell me something,' he murmured. 'Am I right?'

Cavendish started.

'What makes you think that?' he asked.

The dramatist shrugged his shoulders.

'Your manner,' he answered.

'Well, you're quite right.' The other leaned towards him. 'I've been thinking it over all day, and I — I feel I ought to tell someone, and I'd rather it was you than the police. I — I *did* come down here to see Venita Shayne.'

'I never doubted it for a moment,' answered Lowe calmly.

'And I saw her,' went on Cavendish, speaking rapidly. 'I saw her on the Friday night.'

Lowe had not been prepared for this. He stared.

'On the Friday night?' he repeated. 'When?'

'After everybody had gone to bed,' said Cavendish. 'I don't know the exact time, about two o'clock, I think. It was so hot I couldn't sleep, and I came down to the river. It was almost as light as day with the moon, and looking across I saw Venita on the lawn in a bathing costume and I swam across.'

'What was she doing on the lawn at that hour?' demanded the dramatist.

Cavendish shook his head.

'I don't know,' he answered. 'I didn't ask her.' He was nervous and ill at ease, twisting a cigarette between his fingers.

'Go on,' said the dramatist. 'You've something else to say haven't you?'

'Yes.' The other nodded. 'I've this to say. You think I came down here because I was in love with Venita, don't you? I wasn't! I hated her! I came down here because I was hoping to persuade her to break off the engagement between us!'

12

Cavendish Speaks

It took a great deal to surprise Trevor Lowe but he was surprised now. Not only surprised but a little shocked. The other's statement went a long way to confirm Inspector Cotter's theory.

'I think,' he said, after a slight pause, 'you'd better tell me everything. Half confidences are dangerous.'

'I've already decided to,' said Cavendish. 'As I say, I've been thinking the matter over today, and it seems to me that I'm in rather a dangerous position. I've got an idea that inspector fellow suspects me.'

'Naturally your presence requires an explanation,' said the dramatist, evading a direct reply. 'Your original story was rather difficult to swallow.'

'Yes, I know.' Cavendish struck a match and lighted the cigarette he had been fiddling with. 'The whole thing's rather difficult, I don't like talking about it, particularly as Venita's dead, but for my own sake I feel you ought to know.'

He drew several jerky puffs at his cigarette and then went on:

'I daresay you feel surprised when I tell you I hated Venita considering that I was engaged to her. But the engagement was not of my seeking. She forced me into it!'

'Forced you into it?' said Lowe in surprise. 'How?'

'By threatening to disclose something she knew about me to my father,' answered Cavendish.

Lowe pursed up his lips in a silent whistle. Here was a distinctly unpleasant light on the character of the dead girl, if the man before him was speaking the truth. Here, also was a dangerous admission, which, if it came to the ears of Inspector Cotter, would result in the immediate arrest of Cavendish on a charge of murder.

'Are you serious?' he said quietly.

'I'm quite serious,' answered Cavendish. 'I know it's hard believe. To most people Venita presented the appearance of rather a sweet, doll-like little thing, but they didn't know her. She was shrewd, hard as iron, and completely unmoral. I don't mean that in the accepted sense of the term,' he added hastily. 'I mean, if she set her heart on a thing she didn't mind how she got it. And she set her heart on marrying a title. She told me so quite frankly. It was the one thing necessary to complete her ambition. I don't know whether you know, but father is an invalid. It's doubtful if he can live very much longer, and when he dies, of course I inherit the title and the estate.

'Venita fancied herself as Lady Glenriven, and since she had in her possession means to achieve her object she didn't hesitate to use them.'

'What were these means?' asked Lowe; and the other hesitated. 'You'd better be quite frank, Mr. Cavendish,' said the dramatist.

'Well, they were — they were letters,' said the young man. 'Some years ago I fell rather heavily for a girl who, well, she wasn't free. She was married to a man much older than herself, a disagreeable blighter, as jealous as hell. There was nothing in it really, but we wrote rather stupid letters to each other. Somehow or other, she wouldn't tell me how, Venita got hold of these. She threatened to send copies of them to my father and copies of them to the husband unless I did what she asked. I wasn't so much afraid of father knowing as I was of getting the girl into trouble. It would have been a terrible scandal, a divorce that would have affected one of the best-known names in England. In fact trouble all around.

'I had to agree to Venita's terms. She said she'd give me the letters for a wedding present if I would become engaged to her. I agreed. There was nothing else I could do. But I asked her for the present to keep the engagement secret. She wasn't very pleased at this, but she reluctantly consented. That's why I was so astonished when you told me she'd announced it here at dinner.

'That's what brought me down here. I wanted to see her and try and plead with her to drop the wretched business.'

'And when you saw her on the Friday night,' asked Lowe, 'what did she say?'

'She laughed at me!' said Cavendish. 'Told me it was no use trying to get out of my bargain, that if I did she'd carry out her threat. She told me that she was very annoyed at my coming to the island, and that I'd better leave first thing in the morning. That's why I asked you not to say anything to Venita, you remember?'

Lowe nodded.

'I was hoping,' went on Cavendish, 'to get another opportunity of speaking to her. I'd made up my mind to try every possible means of persuading her to change her mind.'

'I suppose you realize,' said Lowe seriously, 'that you'll have to inform the police about that?'

'Is it necessary?' muttered Cavendish. 'I want to avoid any publicity. Not from my point of view so much as the point of view of the other people concerned.'

'There need be none,' said the dramatist. 'But the police will have to be told. Don't you realize that you've supplied a motive for Venita Shayne's murder, and a very strong one!'

'So far as I'm concerned, d'you mean?'

said the other. 'Because I can assure you, Mr. Lowe, and I'm willing to swear it, that I had no hand in the killing of Venita.'

'Not only as far as you're concerned,' said the dramatist, 'but other people as well. If she went to the length of blackmailing you there's no reason why she shouldn't have done the same with someone else. Not with the same object, of course, but for some other. And that someone else might quite easily have decided that the only way out was the death of the blackmailer.'

'Yes, I see,' muttered the young man. 'Well, I'll be guided by you, Mr. Lowe, but you realize my position.'

'I quite realize it,' said the dramatist, 'and you have my sympathy. D'you think Hammond knew about this?'

Cavendish shook his head.

'I don't think so,' he answered. 'I think she had some hold over Hammond, too. She seemed to be able to make him do just what she wanted.'

'Because I'm convinced,' said Lowe, 'that the person who killed Venita also killed Hammond, and therefore whatever motive applies in one case must also apply in the other.'

He broke off as a figure appeared from the darkness of the lounge. It was Minter, come to clear away the coffee cups. When he had gone Lowe rose to his feet.

'I'm going to sleep on this, Cavendish,' he said. 'It will probably be necessary for you to see Inspector Cotter in the morning and tell him what you've told me.'

'I'll follow whatever advice you like to give,' said Cavendish. 'But I do want to avoid any publicity.'

'Tell me one thing,' said Lowe as they entered the house. 'These letters of yours, where did she keep them? We found nothing of the sort at her flat when we searched it this afternoon.'

'She was too cute,' answered Cavendish. 'She kept them at her solicitors. I know that because I asked her once, and she said if I was thinking of trying to get them back by committing burglary I'd have my trouble for nothing. Then she told me where they were.'

They parted in the hall, and Lowe went

up to his room. Arnold was sitting in a chair by the window, glancing through an illustrated magazine.

'Hello!' he said as the dramatist entered. 'What was the idea of shooing me off like that?'

'A very good idea,' said his employer, 'as it turned out. I had a feeling that Cavendish wanted to speak to me about something, and I was right. He did!'

He repeated to the astonished secretary the gist of the conversation.

'Nice little lady!' commented White. 'I'm beginning to think the person who strangled her did quite a number of people a good turn!'

'So am I!' said Lowe grimly. 'There's nothing more detestable than blackmail. In my opinion it's worse than murder.'

'It looks bad for Cavendish,' said Arnold. 'He had the opportunity and the motive.'

'Yes, I'll agree,' said the dramatist. 'But I don't somehow see him in the part of our murderer.'

'Cotter won't bother whether he sees him or not!' grunted White. 'He'll pinch him right away!'

129

'I'm afraid you're right,' said Lowe. 'But Cotter will have to be told. Cavendish knows that. We can't keep important evidence like that secret.'

'I wonder what Venita Shayne was doing on the lawn,' muttered the secretary, 'at two o'clock in the morning?'

'I've been wondering that, too,' said Lowe. 'But what I'm wondering mostly at the moment is the explanation for that mark on her arm. I've got an idea if we could find how that came about we'd know a lot more than we do now.'

White left him soon after, but tired though he was the dramatist did not go to bed immediately. Pulling up a chair to the open window he sat down and thought over all the information that was in his possession, trying to sort it out so that it would make a coherent pattern.

When he failed in this he came back to the burn. What had caused that mark?

He had given it up and was preparing to get into bed when suddenly, from nowhere it seemed, the simple explanation came to him. He stood rigid, one arm in the sleeve of his pyjama jacket, his eyes narrowed.

That was it! That *must* be it!

Well, it wouldn't be difficult to prove. He determined, if the conditions were favourable, to make the experiment on the following day.

13

Trevor Lowe Tries an Experiment

Lowe was up early on the Monday morning, and the first thing he did after getting out of bed was to go to the window and anxiously inspect the weather. There was every promise of the heat wave continuing, and he gave a little grunt of satisfaction. It was necessary, in order to try out the idea which had occurred to him on the previous night, that everything should be as near a replica of the Saturday afternoon on which Venita had been killed as possible.

He shaved, had his bath, and dressed and went down to breakfast. Arnold was the only one up, and he and his employer had breakfast together on the loggia. After the meal Lowe notified Minter that he would not be back until lunch and set out for a solitary ramble round the district.

The test which would prove whether

his theory to account for the burn on the dead woman's arm was the right one could not be tried out until the afternoon, and he had much to think about in the meanwhile.

With his hands in his pockets and a pipe clenched between his teeth he strode leisurely along, passing through the village of Bray, and striking out into the open country beyond. The questions that had to be answered were many, and as he walked he tabulated them mentally.

Why had Marjorie Lovelace and Mrs. Hammond hated Venita Shayne? For hated her they had. He remembered the vindictiveness behind the girl's remark when he had first been introduced to her on the Friday afternoon, and the blaze that had come into Mrs. Hammond's eyes at dinner. Why had Hammond been afraid of the dead woman as his wife had suggested? Was this a fact, or was it merely Mrs. Hammond's imagination? Who was the man whom Hammond had detected watching him, and for what reason had this surveillance been carried out? Why had somebody gone to the trouble of breaking into Venita's flat in order to steal her diary? And who was the man called Joe whom the maid had described as 'looking like a bank clerk'? What connection between the murders had the anonymous letters, and who had sent them? What was the significance of the crude drawing of the dangling man, which took the place of a signature? And what was Venita Shayne doing on the lawn of Backwaters at two o'clock in the morning?

It was a formidable list, and Lowe made a wry face. Perhaps some of the questions would answer themselves as more information concerning the dead girl's past came to light. There was another thing, too. Why had Hammond kept that marriage certificate so carefully? Who were Molly Dwyer and James Hinkley, and what interest had the dead producer had in their marriage?

There were depths to this case that made it unique, depths that might prove to be full of unpleasant things.

Venita Shayne herself, if Cavendish had spoken the truth, was not a very pleasant character. A woman who would blackmail a man into an engagement was capable of anything. Neither had the sour-faced maid been particularly enthusiastic concerning her mistress. Yet Eric Norman had eulogised her to the sky, but then Eric Norman had been in love with her, there was no doubt of that. Lowe had been convinced of it when he had seen the reception that the press agent had accorded to the announcement of her engagement. He had tried cleverly to hide his feelings, but the expression in his eyes had given him away. So naturally his estimation of her character was prejudiced. Hammond, too, may have been afraid of her, but he was certainly fond of her. He had been genuinely cut up at her death.

The queer business was beset with currents and cross currents. The dramatist thought that buried deeply beneath the surface was something particularly nasty. The spade of the investigators would bring to light strange and unclean things. There was a stirring in the mud that hinted at revelations unsuspected, dark and sinister shapes that had long been hidden.

There was much to be done, he

thought grimly, before the truth could be laid bare. Perhaps his experiment in the afternoon would help. The door of the study had been locked and the key taken away by Inspector Cotter, and since he would need this he called in at the police station on his way back.

Cotter made no demur on handing it over, but he was intensely curious to know why it was wanted.

'Come up to the house at four o'clock this afternoon and perhaps I'll have something to tell you,' said Lowe. 'Until then I'd rather not say anything. There's a possibility the idea I'm working on may be wrong, and I don't want to explain it until I'm sure.'

'We've got in touch with Mr. Hammond's lawyers,' said Cotter. 'Crandal and Peek, of Shaftesbury Avenue. Mr. Peek is coming down to Backwaters this evening.'

'He may be able to supply some useful information,' said Lowe. 'What about the bank?'

'I've seen the manager of the branch in Bray,' said the inspector, 'and he knows very little about Hammond's private affairs.

He only had a subsidiary account there. His main account was at the Capital and Southern in Piccadilly, and I'm making arrangements to see the manager there tomorrow.'

'Did you learn anything concerning the cheque for the hundred and fifty pounds?' inquired the dramatist.

Cotter shook his head.

'Nothing that's going to help us,' he answered. 'It was drawn to 'self' and was endorsed by Hammond. The manager remembered it because it was an unusual amount. Hammond very seldom drew cheques for large amounts on the Bray account, mostly housekeeping bills and tradesmen's accounts. He kept very little floating balance. When he issued a cheque on the Bray branch he covered it with one drawn from the Capital and Southern. It was more or less a convenience account.'

'I see,' murmured the dramatist. 'I should very much like to know, Cotter, what happened to that hundred and fifty pounds.'

'It's going to be next to impossible to trace,' said the inspector. 'Hammond drew it out in pound notes.'

Lowe looked up quickly.

'Oh, he did?' he said. 'That's rather enlightening.'

'You mean,' remarked Cotter shrewdly, 'that he wanted to avoid the possibility of the money being traced?'

Lowe nodded. 'Yes,' he said, 'or the person to whom he gave it insisted it should be in untraceable notes.'

'We've no proof,' muttered the inspector, 'that the money went to anyone. Hammond may have drawn it out for his own use.'

'In which case,' said the dramatist, 'he would hardly have taken it in such a bulky form. If you remember, the money we found in his safe was in fivers and tens. A hundred and fifty pounds in pound notes takes up a lot of room.'

The inspector shrugged his shoulders.

'Well, whoever had it is not likely to come forward,' he said, 'and that's the only way we can trace it.'

'Still, it's worth remembering,' said Lowe, as he rose to take his leave. 'It may be important.'

'I don't think it has any bearing on this business,' said Cotter. 'You know my opinion, Mr. Lowe, and I haven't altered it. Cavendish is the fellow, and as soon as I've got a little more evidence I'm going to put him 'inside'!'

'Well, you must please yourself,' said the dramatist. 'Though personally I think you're wrong.' He remembered what Cavendish had told him on the previous night, and wondered what Cotter would say when he heard of it, as he would have to. It would go a long way towards substantiating his theory.

He returned to Backwaters in time for lunch. Mrs. Hammond was still keeping to her bed and the shadow over the house had not lifted. John Moore was still a little sullen at the restrictions placed upon his liberty, but Marjorie Lovelace had brightened a little and she and Cavendish chatted quite normally. The young man still looked a little harassed, but he seemed in better spirits since he had unburdened himself to Lowe. Eric Norman was still grave, though he attempted to take an interest in Lowe's remarks, and generally bear his share of the lunchtime talk.

Although outwardly he appeared calm enough the dramatist was inwardly excited as the time drew nearer for him to make the experiment, which would prove or disprove his idea.

Immediately he had finished coffee he excused himself and went upstairs to his room. White, who saw there was something on his mind, followed in the hope that he would learn what it was. But he quickly discovered that his employer was not in a confidential mood and disappointedly, left him to his own devices.

At half-past two, making sure that he was not observed by any of the household, the dramatist slipped out of his room, went down to the first floor, and unlocking the door of the study let himself in, closing and locking the door behind him. And his subsequent actions were peculiar.

Crossing to the desk he carefully placed a chair in the exact position it had occupied on the previous afternoon when it had held the dead body of Venita

Shayne. When he had done this he seated himself, took off his jacket, and turned up his right shirt sleeve until his arm was bare to the elbow. For a moment his eyes searched the desk keenly, noting the position of every object and mentally comparing it with the picture he had in his mind. When he had satisfied himself that nothing had been moved he leaned forward, shifting about until he was in a similar position to that in which the murdered woman had been found.

And then he remained motionless, his eyes fixed on his watch. At three o'clock he came quietly out of the study, locked the door, and returning the key to his pocket made his way back to his bedroom. His pale face was slightly flushed and there was a brightness in his eyes. For the result of his experiment had been completely successful. On his right forearm was an exactly similar burn to that which had interested him so much in the case of Venita Shayne.

14

The Time of the Crime

Precisely at four o'clock Inspector Cotter arrived and was shown by Minter, who had been notified of his coming, into the lounge where Lowe was waiting to receive him. The big room was empty. Cavendish and Marjorie Lovelace had taken one of the punts on the river, and Arnold White and John Moore had settled themselves with books on the lawn.

'Well,' said Cotter, 'I'm here! Have you got anything to tell me?'

'Yes, I've got a lot to tell you,' said the dramatist.

'You've hit on something, sir?' The inspector eyed him shrewdly.

'I've hit on quite a lot,' admitted Lowe, 'but I don't think we'd better talk here. Come up to the study and I'll tell you all about it.'

He led the way upstairs, and when they

were secure of interruption:

'I think I'm going to surprise you, Cotter,' he said, and to the astonishment of the inspector he took off his coat, rolled up his right shirt sleeve, and showed the amazed official his forearm. 'Take a look at that!' he said quietly.

Cotter's eyes opened wide as he saw the angry, red mark.

'Why — why, it's a burn!' he exclaimed. 'Exactly like that on Miss Shayne's arm. How did you come by it?'

'I came by it,' said Lowe, 'at exactly two-forty-one today.'

'But how — ' began the inspector.

'Wait a minute,' broke in the dramatist, 'and I'll tell you. You know that burn has worried me ever since I saw it on the dead girl's arm. Well, last night while I was puzzling over it the reason for its being there occurred to me. It was really a very simple explanation, and I found it by remembering an experiment I used to do when I was a boy.'

Cotter was obviously bewildered.

'But what bearing has it got — ' he began, but again the other interrupted him.

143

'If you'll wait you'll see,' he said. 'What I remembered was that when the sun's rays are concentrated through a lens on to a piece of paper it is possible to set fire to that piece of paper. Now the sun, during the afternoon, shines directly into this room, and although there is no lens to concentrate its rays there is something that has exactly the same effect.' He pointed to the round, plain glass water bottle on Mr. Hammond's desk.

'Do you mean,' gasped the inspector, 'that that burn was caused by the sun?'

Lowe nodded.

'I do!' he declared. 'And if you haven't already guessed I'll tell you how important it is. I came up here this afternoon and sat at the desk in exactly the same position as that occupied by Venita Shayne when we found her. I bared my arm and I waited. At exactly two-thirty-nine by my watch I experienced a warm, prickly sensation, and saw that the rays of the sun, concentrated through that bottle of water, were impinging on my bare flesh. By *two-forty-one* I had acquired a burn similar in every respect to that on

Miss Shayne's arm.'

Cotter frowned.

'I still don't see what you're trying to get at,' he muttered.

'Don't you?' said the dramatist. 'Well, listen. How long would you sit and bear the pain of a burn if you could move?'

'Good God, Mr. Lowe!' cried the startled inspector, as the other's meaning burst on him. 'You — I see! She was *dead* at the time the burn was made?'

'Yes,' said Lowe. 'That's the only explanation for her sitting calmly while the concentrated rays of the sun bored into her flesh. It's the only sensible explanation, because she had only to move her arm an inch or two and there would have been no burn.'

'But if she was dead at two-forty-one,' said Cotter, 'then the alibis are — '

'Not complete,' finished Lowe triumphantly. 'If she was dead at two-forty-one — we've got of course to allow for a slight difference in the time, because the sun would have taken a little longer to reach the same position today than it did on Saturday, but it would only be a matter of a minute or two — if she was dead at say *two-thirty-nine,* then neither Eric Norman's nor Montague Hammond's alibis hold good. Neither does the maid's evidence nor Minter's that nobody came or went by way of the hall hold good. In fact it opens up immense possibilities.'

'By the Lord Harry, you're right!' exclaimed Cotter, and then frowning suddenly: 'But what about the letter. There's no doubt that was timed at three-fifteen. You're not suggesting it was a forgery?'

'No.' The dramatist shook his head. 'But I think I can offer you an explanation. On Saturday at lunchtime, Miss Shayne complained that her watch had stopped. Apparently it had received a blow of some description. The only time she had to go by was this clock on the desk' — he jerked his head towards it — 'Supposing the crime to have been premeditated, and I'm beginning to think it was, there was nothing to prevent the murderer putting that clock on *before* she entered this room and putting it back to the right time *after* he'd killed her. By that means he would have an alibi for the *false* time of the crime, namely from three-fifteen onwards, but no alibi for the *real* time, which was *before* two-thirty-nine.'

The inspector nodded slowly.

'I must say you've worked it out well,' he admitted. 'We shall have to go into all that evidence again, as far as I can see.'

'A great deal of it will have to be reconsidered,' said Lowe, 'in the light of what we now know. But it means that someone from outside could have entered without being seen, murdered Venita Shayne and escaped. They could have entered at any time prior to two-thirty, set the clock, and escaped immediately after strangling the girl when there was no maid to see them and no Minter in the hall.'

'There's a snag,' said Cotter after a pause. 'There's a snag, Mr. Lowe. If a stranger from outside had committed this murder how did he know that Venita Shayne would be in the study at that time?'

It was a point that Lowe had

overlooked, and he admitted the fact. Venita Shayne had not announced her intention of writing letters until after luncheon.

'Who knew,' went on the inspector, 'that Miss Shayne was coming up here?'

'We all knew,' said Lowe. 'She told the household in general on the terrace when Hammond was asking everyone what they'd like to do during the afternoon.'

'On the terrace, eh?' Cotter's eyes narrowed. 'Then anybody on the island could have heard.'

Lowe saw which way his mind was drifting, but he was forced to agree.

'You know how clearly voices carry over water, Mr. Lowe,' said the inspector. 'It acts as a sort of sound conductor. Cavendish could have heard, and therefore my theory about his swimming across and coming up by the path behind the roses is even more possible than it was before. And he hadn't even got to dodge Minter.'

Lowe nodded slowly.

'Oh, I agree with you that your theory's possible enough,' he said. 'I'm not arguing about its possibility. It's just that I don't think it's the right one. Certainly if Cavendish killed Venita Shayne his motive wasn't jealousy.'

'You think not?' said Cotter.

'I *know* it wasn't!' retorted Lowe, and repeated the conversation he had had with the young man on the previous night.

Cotter listened interestedly.

'Well, that clinches it, Mr. Lowe!' he declared. 'Absolutely clinches it. It's a bigger motive than the other! He was in the clutches of this woman and he wanted to get out, and the only way to get out was to kill her. He tried to reason with her on the Friday night and she wouldn't listen. It's as plain as a pikestaff!'

'And what about Hammond?' demanded Lowe. 'Why did he kill him?'

'Maybe Hammond was in it,' answered Cotter. 'Probably he and the Shayne girl were working together. She was under contract to Hammond and playing in all his shows, wasn't she? Well, it would have been good publicity if she'd married a title. It all hangs together, Mr. Lowe.' He rose to his feet and began to walk up and down excitedly. 'That's why he pinched her diary. He knew she'd made some reference to the hold she had on him in it. Perhaps she told him she'd mentioned the name of this woman. By gosh!' He stopped and struck his fist into his cupped hand. 'That broken watch! You say he saw her at two o'clock on the lawn. I'll bet what happened was they quarrelled and he grabbed her wrist, breaking the watch. That's what put the idea into his head of altering the time here when he decided that there was nothing left but to kill her. It's a perfect case, sir. I'd take it before any jury!'

The dramatist nodded slowly. There was no doubt that appearances were very black, so far as Cavendish was concerned. As Cotter said, it was almost a perfect case.

'I'll admit you'd be justified in arresting Cavendish,' he said. 'But I've got a feeling, a hunch if you like to call it, that there's something deeper.' He caressed his chin. 'I'm sure he didn't do it!' he declared suddenly.

'Well, you can have your own ideas on the subject, Mr. Lowe,' said Cotter grimly, 'but I'm going to apply for a warrant first thing in the morning, and I don't think I'll be making a mistake.'

The dramatist made no effort to dissuade him. He realised that the inspector was doing no more than his duty. The evidence against Cavendish was strong enough and it was only his own conviction that made him believe in the young man's innocence. And he was to be glad later that he had not interfered, for although Cotter carried out his intention and applied for a warrant something happened during that night which effectually stayed his hand in executing it.

15

What Mr. Peek Knew

Mr. Harrison Peek, the junior partner of Crandle and Peek, the solicitors who had handled Montague Hammond's affairs, arrived at half-past six. He was a youngish, business-like little man, very affable and considerably shocked at the fate that had overtaken his client.

Inspector Cotter, who had returned to the police station at Bray after his conference with Lowe, came back in time to meet the lawyer, and the three of them held a consultation in the lounge.

'I thought it best to come down,' said Mr. Peek. 'It will be necessary for me to see Mrs. Hammond. This is a dreadful affair! The papers are full of it.' He took off his glasses and wiped them vigorously on a silk handkerchief. 'Have you any idea who could have been responsible?'

'We hope to make an arrest shortly,' said Cotter.

'That's very gratifying, very gratifying indeed,' said Mr. Peek. 'May I inquire whom you suspect?'

'I don't think it would be advisable to disclose that at present, sir,' said the inspector.

'No, no, quite! Of course not!' The lawyer nodded wisely. 'Stupid of me to ask. I understand Mrs. Hammond is prostrate? Very natural. Very natural.'

'Was Mr. Hammond a rich man?' inquired Lowe.

The lawyer pursed his lips.

'Well, not exactly rich,' he answered. 'But very well off. Yes, I should say exceedingly well off.'

'What was he worth, roughly, sir?' asked the inspector.

'Well, I haven't had time to go into the matter,' said Mr. Peek, with a glance at the brief bag beside him, 'but I should say, everything combined, he was worth a hundred and fifty thousand pounds!'

Cotter screwed up his lips in a silent whistle.

'As much as that?' he said. 'I should call that rich.'

'He was very successful,' said Mr. Peek. 'His recent productions have all made money.'

'How long have you been acting for him?' inquired the dramatist, and the lawyer considered.

'A considerable number of years,' he replied, after a pause. 'Let me see now. Yes, it must be getting on for seventeen.'

'Did you handle his private as well as his business affairs?' went on Lowe.

'The majority of them,' said Mr. Peek. 'We looked after such things as insurances, which reminds me, Mr. Hammond was heavily insured.'

'Oh, was he?' said the dramatist, with a gleam of interest.

'To the extent of ten thousand pounds,' went on the lawyer. 'That is one of the things I wish to see Mrs. Hammond about. She benefits.'

'Added to the hundred and fifty thousand pounds?' said the inspector. 'She'll come into a nice little sum then.'

Peek looked a trifle disconcerted.

'Yes,' he admitted. 'In the circumstances she will.'

Lowe eyed him sharply.

'How d'you mean, 'in the circumstances'?' he asked.

The lawyer cleared his throat.

'Well,' he said hesitantly, 'had Miss Shayne still been — er — alive, half of the hundred and fifty thousand pounds would have gone to her. Those are the terms of Mr. Hammond's will.'

'You mean,' said Inspector Cotter, 'that he left his money to be equally divided between Miss Shayne and his wife?'

The lawyer nodded.

'Yes,' he replied. 'But of course, since Miss Shayne predeceased him the full amount will go to the next of kin, which is Mrs. Hammond.'

Lowe frowned. Here was a fresh item of information that was worth consideration. By the death of Venita Shayne and Hammond, Mrs. Hammond had become a rich woman. Had she known of the Will, in which her husband had left half his fortune to the girl? And if she had was this the explanation for the hatred that she had felt for the dead actress?

'When did Mr. Hammond make his will?' he inquired.

'Three years ago,' answered Mr. Peek. 'Shortly after he had first met Miss Shayne.'

'Seems a queer thing to have done,' remarked Inspector Cotter, glancing at Lowe meaningfully. 'He must have been very fond of the lady.'

'I believe he was,' said the lawyer hastily. 'As a matter of fact I myself was a little astonished, and as diplomatically as I could I suggested that he should think the matter over before coming to a final decision. But he wouldn't listen. He insisted upon the will being drawn up immediately and the old one destroyed.'

'The old one left everything to his wife, I presume?' said Lowe.

'Yes,' said Mr. Peek.

The dramatist pulled gently at his lower lip with a thumb and forefinger. It was ridiculous to suspect the gaunt woman upstairs of the murders — but she certainly had a motive. If her opportunity had been equal, the possibility of including her among the list of suspects would have increased.

But the shot that had killed Hammond had, undoubtedly, come from the island, and so far as the death of Venita Shayne was concerned, she had a perfect alibi. From luncheon until the discovery had been made she had never gone inside the house. At the same time this didn't entirely preclude her from knowledge of the murders. There was a possibility she might have been working in conjunction with someone else, someone who had actually carried out the killings.

'Knowing Mr. Hammond so well,' said Lowe, 'you'll be able to tell us something of his private affairs.'

'In what respect?' replied the lawyer with habitual caution.

'Generally,' said the dramatist. 'What sort of man was he?'

'That's rather difficult to answer,' said Mr. Peek, with a faint smile. 'He was a very straight man. Scrupulously honest in all his business dealings. But beyond that I really knew very little about him.'

'Then you wouldn't be in a position to

say whether he had any enemies?' continued Lowe. 'Or whether there was anything in his past history that could have had any bearing on his death?'

'No, I'm afraid I can't.' The lawyer shook his head. 'Certainly there was nothing to my knowledge.'

'Were you aware,' said Lowe, 'that he had been considerably worried recently by the receipt of a number of anonymous letters?'

Mr. Peek looked at him startled.

'No, I was not aware of that,' he answered.

'The last arrived on the morning of the day on which Miss Shayne was killed,' said the dramatist. 'It contained a rather broad hint that something would happen to her.'

'But this is extraordinary!' said Mr. Peek.

'It was signed by the crude drawing of a man dangling on a noose suspended from a gallows,' continued the dramatist. 'Mr. Hammond had had several of them. Some merely abusive, some definitely threatening. He was anxious to avoid any form of publicity and knowing that I have dabbled in such things before, he came to me and asked me to try and discover who was responsible for these epistles. But I am under the impression that he knew. I think he was on the point of telling me when he was killed.'

'He never mentioned the matter to me,' declared the lawyer.

'He was also considerably worried and annoyed,' said Lowe, 'by a man who was apparently keeping him under observation. Did you know anything about that?'

'No. All this is news to me,' said Mr. Peek. 'D'you think it can have any bearing on his death?'

'Personally I think it has a considerable bearing on his death,' answered Lowe. 'And also on the death of Miss Shayne. But exactly how I haven't the least idea. I was hoping that perhaps you would be able to suggest a connection.'

'I'm afraid your hopes are not destined to materialise, sir,' said Mr. Peek. 'I have no more idea than you why anyone should send anonymous letters to Mr. Hammond, or keep him under observation. As I say, though my firm has handled his business affairs, and some of his private ones, for the past seventeen years, we knew very little about Mr. Hammond personally. He was a very reticent man, genial enough on the surface, but very difficult to get to know, if you understand what I mean.'

Lowe nodded. He had experienced something of the same thing himself during his short acquaintance with the dead producer.

'Was he married when he first came to your firm?' he inquired.

'No, no,' said the lawyer. 'He didn't marry until eight years after.'

'Did he ever mention to you anyone of the name of Molly Dwyer, or James Hinkley?' continued Lowe, and once again he drew blank.

'No, I've never heard the names,' said Mr. Peek. 'Why?'

'We discovered a marriage certificate in his safe,' explained the dramatist. 'It was twenty-six years old and it certified that Molly Dwyer, parlour maid, and James Hinkley, actor, were married at the Bloomsbury Registrar's office on April

8th, 1911. It was carefully preserved, and I'm wondering why Hammond should have kept it. His name doesn't appear.'

'Probably the people mentioned were close friends of his, or even relations,' said the puzzled Mr. Peek.

'Yes, probably,' said Lowe. 'And that's another thing I want to ask you. Had Hammond any relations living?'

'That I can answer,' said the lawyer with a smile. 'He had not! His parents died, I believe, when he was quite a youngster, and some years ago an uncle, the only relation he had alive, died, leaving him a small legacy.'

Inspector Cotter had been fidgeting a little impatiently. He saw no reason why time should be wasted with such unnecessary questions. In his own opinion the case was obvious. Lowe, however, was nearly through, and he put his last question.

'I take it,' he said, 'that Mr. Hammond has not always been well off?'

'No,' answered the lawyer. 'At the time he first came to us he was very poor, very poor indeed. It was this legacy that I mentioned which gave him his first start towards success. It was not a very large sum, a matter of two thousand five hundred pounds, but it enabled Mr. Hammond to acquire a play and take it on tour. It was successful and from then on he never looked back.'

There was a tap at the door and Minter entered.

'Excuse me,' he said, 'but Mrs. Hammond would like to see you, sir.'

Mr. Peek rose instantly to his feet.

'Is there anything else you gentlemen would like to ask me?' he inquired.

'Not as far as I'm concerned, sir,' said the inspector, and Lowe shook his head.

'Then I'll go up to Mrs. Hammond at once, said the lawyer, addressing Minter, and with a nod to the others followed the servant out of the room.

'What was at the back of your mind, Mr. Lowe?' said Cotter, when they were alone, 'asking all those questions?'

'Nothing,' answered the dramatist candidly. 'Only the desire for information, which,' — he made a rueful grimace — 'I didn't get.'

'You can take it from me, sir,' declared the inspector emphatically, 'that you're wasting time. You're trying to find something intricate in this case, and there isn't. It's just plain and straightforward.'

'You think so?' said the dramatist. 'Well, I beg to differ, Inspector.'

'Well, we shall see who is right,' said Cotter. 'You'll find I'm right in this case, Mr. Lowe. Cavendish is the fellow, and I'm pulling him in tomorrow.'

He broke off as a sharp, peremptory knocking sounded from the hall. They heard the footsteps of the maid pass the door of the lounge, and the murmur of a man's voice. There was a slight altercation in which Minter's tone could be heard, and then the manservant appeared at the door.

'Excuse me,' he said apologetically, 'but there's a — a person here who — '

So far he got when he was brushed aside and a small, wizened-faced man strode jauntily in.

'Good evenin',' he said in a slightly husky voice, surveying Lowe and the inspector. 'My name's Secket, Joe Secket, and I want to see Mrs. 'Ammond.'

'I've already told you,' said the indignant Minter. 'Mrs. Hammond is ill.'

'Then I want to see someone who's in charge 'ere,' declared the newcomer.

'We are more or less in charge here at the moment,' said Lowe quietly. 'What do you want, Mr. Secket?'

The man looked at them with shrewd little black eyes.

'What do I want?' he echoed. 'Well, I like that! What do I want? I want ter know the ins and outs of this business.'

'What business?' said Lowe sharply.

'This murder,' said the little man truculently. 'This killin' of Venita Shayne. I want to know all about it.'

'And what business is it of yours?' said the dramatist, with a gleam of interest in his eyes.

'Business of mine? I'll tell yer!' said Mr. Secket, thrusting his hands into the pockets of his rather loud suit and staring belligerently at them. 'I'll tell you wot business it is of mine. Venita Shayne was my wife!'

16

Exit Mr. Secket

Trevor Lowe had more or less expected something of the sort, but all the same he stared in astonishment at the uncouth figure of the man before him. Venita Shayne's husband! The man was loud-voiced and common, the last person in the world one would have associated with the delicately nurtured Venita. And yet there was a confidence in his bearing that convinced the dramatist he was speaking the truth. This, then, was the mysterious Joe whom the maid had mentioned as having been one of the few constant visitors to the girl's flat.

Inspector Cotter stared in equal amazement, although his surprise was more evident than Lowe's. His mouth had dropped half open and his eyes were wide.

Mr. Secket surveyed them, an unpleasant expression on his narrow face.

'Give yer a bit of a shock, ain't it?' he remarked. 'I'm not surprised. I bet it 'ud give a lot of people a shock. But there it is, and I've got the marriage certificate to prove it! Married in Wigan we were, six years ago, an' a proper mess-up it was. Blimey! What a little — '

'That 'ull do!' said Lowe sharply. 'Why have you come here, Mr. Secket?'

'Why have I come here?' The little man seemed to have a habit of repeating everything. 'Why 'ave I come 'ere? Ain't it natural that 'er lawful 'usband should come and want to know who did in 'is wife? Besides,' he added, 'anythin' that belonged to 'er is mine now. I'm the next of kin, see?'

'But I still don't see why you came here,' said the dramatist. 'Why didn't you go to Miss Shayne's lawyers?'

'Miss Shayne! Why don't you call 'er by 'er proper name? Mrs. Secket! Why didn't I go to 'er lawyers? Because I don't 'old with lawyers, see. This is where she was killed, wasn't it? Well, I've come 'ere to look after things.' He pushed his bowler hat to the back of his head. 'Joe Secket ain't the type to sit quiet and let somebody do 'im out of 'is rights! I was 'er 'usband and I'm the rightful chap to see that everything's square and above-board.'

'You seem to have been a long time making up your mind,' remarked Lowe dryly.

'Watcher mean?' said Mr. Secket.

'I mean,' said the dramatist, 'that you kept this marriage pretty secret, didn't you?'

'She insisted on it,' answered the man. 'Ashamed o' me, she was. Ashamed o' me!'

Looking at him Lowe was not altogether surprised. Supposing his statement to be true the alliance must have been embarrassing to a girl of Venita Shayne's fame and position.

'Ashamed of 'er own 'usband! What d'you think of that?' continued Mr. Secket in an injured voice. 'That'll show you what sort of girl she was. And after me rescuing 'er from starvation, too.'

'I presume,' said Lowe, a little sternly, 'that Miss Shayne was not altogether ungenerous in return for your — er — discretion?'

'How d'you mean?' inquired the man. 'What yer gettin' at?'

'I mean,' said the dramatist, 'that no doubt she paid you well to keep your — er — your relationship secret.'

'Five quid a week!' said Mr. Secket disgustedly. 'Five quid a week! And look at all the money she was earnin'. And me, who picked 'er out of the gutter!'

'How did you come to meet Miss Shayne?' put in Cotter.

'Stranded she was,' explained Mr. Secket. 'Got left at 'Ull. Manager of the show she was with, did a bunk and left the 'ole crowd. Nita couldn't pay 'er digs nor nothin'.'

'Are we to understand,' said Lowe, 'that you were also in the — er — profession?'

'Baggage man and carpenter,' said Mr. Secket promptly. 'And there weren't a better on the road, you can ask anyone. And what'll they tell you?'

The dramatist did not trouble to inquire. His interest was centred on this man's connection with the dead girl.

'I don't know that we can do anything for you,' he said. 'If you want to make any claim you must do so through Miss Shayne's solicitors. At the same time, now you are here you might just as well answer a few questions.'

Mr. Secket eyed him suspiciously.

'What d'you mean, questions?' he demanded.

'A certain amount of mystery surrounds the death of — er — of your wife,' said Lowe. 'Perhaps you can help us.'

'Me?' The word exploded from Mr. Secket's mouth in a startled gasp. 'I know nothin' about it! Now look here, mister, don't you go imaginin' that I 'ad anythin' to do with it. I wasn't near the place.'

'Nobody's suggesting that you were,' said the dramatist sharply. 'I'm merely asking if you know anything that might assist us in finding the murderer.'

'I don' know nothin'!' the answer came swiftly. 'Nothin' at all!'

Lowe's eyes narrowed. In his opinion Mr. Secket seemed altogether too eager to affirm his lack of knowledge.

'Did Miss Shayne ever mention to you

that she was afraid of anyone?' he prompted.

'Afraid of anyone!' Mr. Secket sniffed. 'You don't know Nita! She weren't afraid of no one, not even the Devil 'imself! But there was quite a number of people who was afraid of 'er,' he added.

'Oh, were there?' snapped Inspector Cotter. 'Who?'

Mr. Secket looked a little uneasy.

'I wasn't meanin' anyone in particular,' he mumbled. 'I was just speakin' generally.'

'But you must have had some reason,' said Lowe. 'What made you think that people were afraid of Venita Shayne?'

'Well quite a lot of 'em were,' said the man defiantly. 'That feller 'Ammond was, fer one. I don't know what 'old she 'ad on 'im, but she used to boast that anythin' she wanted he'd have to do. And there was another feller, a lord or somethin'. She'd got 'im taped, too.'

'Are you referring to Mr. Cavendish?' said the inspector.

'That's the chap!' Secket nodded.

'Did you know Mr. Cavendish?' asked Lowe.

'No blinkin' fear!' answered the little

man. 'You don't suppose Nita would 'ave introduced me to any of her swell friends, do yer?'

'Then you were not aware,' continued the dramatist, 'that your — er — wife was trying to force Mr. Cavendish into a marriage.'

Obviously this was news to Mr. Secket, for his jaw dropped and his eyes bulged.

'Blimey, was she now?' he exclaimed. 'So that was 'er little game, was it? Bigamy, eh? And she used to threaten me with . . . ' He stopped abruptly.

Lowe's eyes glinted.

'Oh, she threatened you, did she?' he said softly. 'Now what did she threaten you with, Mr. Secket?'

'It was a figger of speech,' said Secket quickly. 'I didn't mean nothin'.' He shifted his feet uncomfortably.

'Oh yes, you did!' said the dramatist. 'You meant exactly what you said. Now what did Venita Shayne threaten you with, and why? I know!' he said suddenly as it came to him. 'She threatened you with something to prevent you revealing the fact that you and she were married. Is that it?'

''Ere, who told you that?' cried Secket in alarm. 'Did she tell you that?'

'Nobody told me,' said Lowe. 'But it's obvious. You gave yourself away. Now what did she know about you?'

'She didn't know nothin' about me,' said the other. 'There weren't anythin' in it, really. But it might 'ave caused a lot of trouble. It was while we was on tour. The theatre box office was broken into and a lot of the advance bookin' money taken. She saw me comin' away from the buildin' where I'd been mendin' a bit of scenery on the stage. That week I'd won a bit o' money on a 'orse which I 'adn't told 'er about and I was a bit flush. She jumped to conclusions.' Mr. Secket became indignant. 'Naturally it wasn't nothin' to do with me. I didn't touch the money. I wouldn't do such a thing. You ask anyone, my reputation's good, it is!'

'I see,' said Lowe. 'Oh, well, we won't go into that.' So this was the reason the man had been so willing to hush up his marriage with the famous Venita Shayne. She had used the knowledge that she possessed concerning this robbery to force him to keep silent.

The more he learned about the dead girl's character the less he liked it. Venita Shayne had evidently not been a nice person.

'And what were you doing, Mr. Secket,' broke in Inspector Cotter, 'between the hours of two and four-thirty last Saturday afternoon?'

'What was I doin'?' Secket switched his eyes from Lowe to the speaker. ''Ere, what's the little game, eh? What you a tryin' ter do? Pull a fast one, eh?'

'Suppose you answer Inspector Cotter's question,' said Lowe sternly.

'Who?' There was naked fear in the man's eyes now. 'Inspector Cotter? Is 'e a pleeceman? Gor' blimey! I've dropped into a nice pickle, I 'ave!'

'Tell us where you were on Saturday afternoon,' said the dramatist inexorably.

'I wasn't anywhere near 'ere, I give you my word I wasn't!' said Mr. Secket, all his bounce and bluster evaporated.

'Well, where were you?' persisted Lowe. 'It's a simple question, answer it?'

'It ain't as simple as you think,'

muttered Secket. 'I was out. I went for a walk across 'Ampstead 'Eath. I've got digs at Camden Town and — '

'And you were alone, I suppose?' said Lowe.

'Yes. Look 'ere, you don't think I croaked 'er, do yer?' The man's voice was anxious, his eyes restless, and his fingers twitched as they plucked nervously at the bottom of his jacket.

'We suspect everybody,' said Lowe, 'who had a motive. And you had a very good one. Venita Shayne was your wife. At her death everything she possessed goes to you, unless she'd made a will.'

'She'd made no will,' put in Secket quickly, and realised his mistake.

'Then everything does go to you,' flashed Lowe. 'Which means that you had a motive for killing her. And you can't account for your movements on Saturday afternoon. You can only say you were out alone on Hampstead Heath.'

'I — I swear it's the truth!' The man's face was damp with perspiration and had turned a pallid, sickly hue. 'It's the truth as sure as I'm standin' 'ere! It was 'ot and

I walked up to 'Ampstead 'Eath and sat under a tree.'

'We've only your word for that,' said Inspector Cotter sternly. 'For all we know you might have been here.'

Mr. Secket licked his suddenly dry lips.

'I wasn't within miles,' he muttered. 'It ain't me you want, it's that feller Cavendish. 'E was 'ere.'

'How do you know that?' snapped Lowe, and Mr. Secket's terror and confusion increased until it was pitiful.

'I — I — ' he stammered, and stopped, gasping like a newly landed fish.

'How do you know Mr. Cavendish was here?' repeated Lowe. 'The only way you could know was because you saw him!'

'I've told yer — ' began Secket huskily.

'A lot of lies!' said the dramatist curtly. 'A lot of lies, Secket! You were here on Saturday afternoon. You never went to Hampstead Heath! Now come on, admit it!'

But Mr. Secket had found a remnant of courage.

'I wasn't here and you can't prove it!' he snarled. 'Don't you go tryin' to frame me! You've no right to put questions like that under the act, and you know it!' His pale face flushed and he glared from one to the other defiantly.

'You sound as if you'd had experience, Mr. Secket,' said Lowe coldly.

'I know the law,' said Secket, 'and I'm not stoppin' 'ere to be put through no third degree. I'm off!' He moved towards the door.

'One moment,' said Cotter. 'We may want you. What's your address?'

The man paused.

'240, Rice Street, Camden Town,' he said suddenly.

'No doubt you have a letter or something on you that will substantiate that,' put in Lowe smoothly, and Inspector Cotter, in the act of noting down the address, paused.

'Can't you take my word for it?' demanded Mr. Secket.

'I should prefer something a little more — substantial,' murmured the dramatist.

'Oh, you would, eh?' Secket plunged his hand into his breast pocket, produced a crumpled mass of papers, selected a letter and extracting the contents threw the envelope on the floor. 'There y'are,' he said. 'Take a look at that! You're so darned suspicious.'

Lowe stooped and picked it up. It was addressed to Joe Secket at the address he had mentioned.

'Thank you,' he said, and put it in his pocket.

The man glared at him, opened his lips to say something, thought better of it, and went out, slamming the door. In two strides the dramatist was out on the loggia. He whistled softly and Arnold White, who was sitting on the lawn, looked round. Lowe beckoned to him, and the secretary came quickly.

'Listen,' said his employer. 'I've got a job of work for you. There's a man just been here called Joe Secket. He's leaving now. You can't mistake him. Follow him wherever he goes.'

White nodded briskly, crossed the room, and slipped out into the hall.

'Do you think that's necessary, Mr. Lowe?' asked the inspector.

'I think it's very necessary,' replied the

dramatist. 'Take a look at that envelope.'
He took it from his pocket and held it
out.

Cotter, with a puzzled frown, glanced
at it.

'I don't see anything,' he remarked.
'Except that it's addressed in capitals.'

'Exactly!' said Lowe. 'And the person
who wrote it is the same person who sent
those anonymous letters to Montague
Hammond and myself!'

17

In the Night

Trevor Lowe sat at the open window of his bedroom smoking thoughtfully. Mr. Peek had left after his interview with Mrs. Hammond, refusing that lady's suggestion that he should stay to dinner.

The evening had passed uneventfully enough, although the day had certainly not been lacking in producing a mild sensation. The advent of Mr. Secket had been both unexpected and interesting.

What had brought him to Backwaters in the first place? The dramatist entirely discounted his own explanation. He had not come for the purpose he had stated. He was a shrewd, cunning little man, without a great deal of intelligence, it was true, but sufficient to know that the proper quarter to make his claim was Venita Shayne's lawyers. So why had he come to Backwaters?

Lowe had a lurking suspicion that he had come to satisfy his curiosity concerning something, but what that something was he had no idea. The reason he had given had been merely an excuse, plausible enough on the surface in view of his relationship with the dead woman, but not plausible enough to withstand an analysis. And what had he been doing in the vicinity of the house on that Saturday afternoon? For that he had been somewhere near Lowe was convinced.

The whole business was very involved. There were so many people who had had a motive for killing Venita Shayne. Mrs. Hammond, Cavendish, this man Secket. His was the strongest of all. And yet the dramatist couldn't quite see him in the role of a killer. The crime had been too cleverly carried out. Secket would never have thought of the time element.

He stared into the hot, airless darkness of the night, his brows drawn together. It was peculiar the mystery that surrounded both the early life of Hammond and also that of the dead girl. That part of their existence seemed to be enveloped in an impenetrable veil of secrecy, and it was behind that veil, he believed, the truth lay. One thing certainly had emerged, and that was the unpleasantness of Venita Shayne's character. Without a doubt the girl had been completely unscrupulous, using any means that lay to her hand to gain her own ends. She had blackmailed Cavendish, she had blackmailed her own husband. She had, apparently, held something over the head of Montague Hammond, and she had obviously been prepared to go to the length of committing bigamy. Altogether a nasty piece of work, a very nasty piece of work, thought Lowe as he puffed slowly at his pipe.

How many other people had she terrified into submission to her desires? Perhaps her lawyers would be of assistance there. Cotter had arranged an appointment with them for the following afternoon, and Lowe was accompanying him. Perhaps they would learn something. There was her bank, too. She had apparently boasted to Cavendish that she had kept the letters that concerned him, at her solicitors. Possibly there were other documents also.

It was an intricate business, full of twists and turns and side issues. Those anonymous letters with the crude drawing of the dangling man — how did they come into it? And the stealing of Venita Shayne's diary? And what had the girl been doing on the lawn at two o'clock on the Saturday morning when Cavendish had seen her and swum over from the island? She hadn't been there to see him, she was not aware that he was in the vicinity. Had she merely been hot and sleepless and gone out for a breath of air? Or had there been some other reason? Had she gone to keep an appointment made previously? Cavendish had seen no one, but the person, whoever it was, may have already been and gone, or arriving and seeing the girl with someone else slipped away. Could — A thought occurred to him. Could this person be Secket, and if so why had he come?

He remembered the dented watch and Cotter's suggested explanation. That Cavendish had been responsible he did not believe. Whatever he may have thought, however much he may have hated the girl, he was not the type to resort to violence. But that damaged watch pointed clearly to someone having gripped her wrist hard. And that sounded more like Secket. It was in keeping with the man's character, it was the sort of thing he would do in an argument.

Lowe yawned. It was getting on for two and he had been sitting by the window thinking for over two hours. He rose to his feet, stretching his stiff limbs. The night was still and silent and unpleasantly hot. He had been sitting in the dark, finding it an aid to the concentration of his thoughts. But now, having made up his mind to undress and go to bed, he reached out his hand towards the lamp. His fingers had touched the switch when he stopped, rigid, listening.

A board had creaked somewhere in the sleeping house!

The dramatist slipped off his shoes and crept noiselessly to the door. Cautiously he turned the handle and opened it a few inches. Everything was silent. Perhaps the sound he had heard meant nothing. In the stillness of the night houses did, occasionally, emit strange noises, and —

The creak came again, faintly but unmistakable. This time from the direction of the staircase.

Silently as a ghost Lowe slipped out into the dark corridor and felt his way along the wall towards the landing. And now he knew he had not been mistaken. Somebody was moving in the darkness below, moving stealthily but unable to prevent the faint creaking of the floor beneath their weight.

He reached the head of the staircase and peered over. The hall was in pitch darkness and he could see nothing. He heard a faint click and a thread of light gleamed for an instant.

He began very carefully to descend the stairs, testing each tread. He could hear vague movements as the unknown prowler went about his mysterious business, whatever it was. He came to the last stair and stood in the hall straining his ears. There was a faint sound from the lounge and rapidly and silently the dramatist glided across the hall to the closed door.

It was open an inch and the faintest glimmer of light showed through the crack. He could hear the sound of movement within, the soft shuffling of feet. There came a gentle thud and a muttered imprecation. Stooping he applied an eye to the keyhole, but he could see nothing but the broad back of a chair.

Rising noiselessly to his feet he hesitated. The sounds had ceased. Either the unknown occupant had left by way of the window or he was standing still.

He moved the door gently, pushing it inwards slowly and carefully. He was determined if possible to find out who was alert and wakeful in that sleeping house.

By slow degrees the gap between the edge of the door and the jamb widened. Another two inches and there would be sufficient room for him to see within. He pressed himself up close against the frame and very cautiously craned forward. The lounge was dim and shadowy, looking abnormally large in the faint light from a candle, which stood on the top of a low bookshelf, and it was empty!

The dramatist squeezed himself round the edge of the door and as he did so it seemed to him that the roof collapsed.

A violent blow caught him on the side of the head. For an infinitesimal moment of time he was conscious of an agonising pain, which seemed to burn up his brain, and then the pain vanished and he felt nothing . . .

18

The Third Victim

Trevor Lowe opened his eyes and blinked dazedly, wondering vaguely why his head ached and the reason for the sense of discomfort that he experienced. The bed seemed exceptionally hard and he was unpleasantly aware of a soreness in his right arm. He moved gingerly. What on earth had happened?

There was a light somewhere — and then memory came back to him. Of course he had been on the point of entering the lounge when something struck him on the head. He was still in the lounge, lying on the hard floor just within the open doorway, and the light came from the flickering candle, which still stood on the edge of the bookcase.

The person who had been in that room must have become aware of his presence. Probably had seen the door move. The reason it had looked empty was because the occupant had come silently over to the door and stood behind it, awaiting his chance. But who was the occupant, and for what reason had he been prowling about in the darkness of the night?

Lowe sat up, and the movement sent a twinge of pain through his head and for an instant made everything swim dizzily. The faintness cleared off after a moment and tenderly he felt the top of his scalp. It was sore, but so far as he could judge the skin had not been broken. There was no blood, he examined the tips of his fingers.

He edged himself towards the back of a big easy chair that stood near, and by its aid got to his feet. He was still feeling pretty groggy. The blow had been a heavy one, and it had caught him completely unawares. He rubbed his arm, which was painful — in falling he must have struck it against the skirting — and looked about him.

The appearance of the lounge was normal, except for the lighted candle on the bookcase. What, then, had the intruder been doing? Why had he come stealthily to this room in the middle of the night?

Lowe's head still ached but his senses were normal. He moved over to the place where the candle stood, but there was no indication of the reason for the marauder's presence.

Glancing about he saw something lying on the floor, and going over he picked it up. It was a heavy, bronze bookend and he looked at it frowning. Evidently this was the weapon that the unknown had used to strike him down. A nasty thing in the hands of a desperate man. It was lucky, he thought grimly, that he had got off as lightly as he had. Obviously none of the rest of the household had heard anything. The place was still silent.

He crossed over and peered through the windows on to the loggia. The darkness was beginning to disperse before the first tinge of dawn. He looked at his watch. It was a quarter to four. He must have been unconscious for some time, time enough, anyway, for the person who was responsible for that blow to have returned to their room. But why had they ever left it? What lay behind that midnight activity?

He stood thoughtfully in the centre of the lounge, gently massaging the sore place on his skull. It seemed a stupid thing for anyone to have taken the trouble to stealthily leave their room and come down to the lounge for no apparent reason. Nothing, so far as he could see, had been disturbed. The windows were latched and fastened. Only the candle showed that anyone had been there at all.

The candle! That might supply a clue to the identity of the night walker. He examined it and quickly discovered that he was wrong. It supplied no clue. It had been taken from the mantelpiece, was one of a pair of silver candlesticks containing four coloured candles, which matched the furnishings of the room.

Lowe was uneasy. There was something sinister about this inexplicable wandering in the night. Had the person been abroad for any lawful purpose they would not have attacked him. The reason they were up and about while the whole house slept was, therefore, for some sinister purpose

190

of their own. But what? And why the visit to the lounge?

That puzzled him considerably. Had they been looking for something? And had he disturbed them before they could conduct the search? That might be the explanation. But what had they been looking for? There was nothing in this big room except a few books, a number of divans and chairs. Not even a writing desk where some paper might have been hidden.

He had picked up the bronze bookend with his handkerchief, and now he carefully wrapped the linen round it. There might be fingerprints there to prove the identity of his attacker. He took the candlestick, holding it carefully by the rim at the top, and moved over to the door. It was no good standing about in that gloomy room wondering. He might as well collect what possible evidence there was and return to his own.

He crossed the gloomy hall and began cautiously to ascend the staircase. He reached his bedroom without hearing a sound or seeing anyone, and carefully setting the candlestick and the bookend down on the table near the bed switched on the light. Cotter would be able to test for prints in the morning. He blew out the candle, removed it from the sconce, and put the bookend and the candlestick carefully away in a drawer.

Turning on the tap and filling the basin with cold water he took off his coat, collar and tie, and bathed his face. A lump was rising on the side of his head but an examination of it in the mirror showed him that little damage had been done. Undressing he got into bed with a sigh of relief, resting his aching head against the pillows gratefully.

But it was a long time before he fell asleep. Staring at the white ceiling he lay trying to puzzle out a solution to the events of the night.

The sky was crimson with the coming sunrise before he finally switched out the light and snuggling down fell asleep . . .

The sound of hurried movements and excited voices roused him, as it seemed, almost before he had closed his eyes. Somebody banged violently on his door and he remembered that he had locked it before turning in.

Getting out of bed he slipped on a dressing gown, went over, and turned the key. Minter, his face pale and frightened, burst into the room without ceremony and without apology.

'The mistress,' he blurted incoherently; 'The mistress — '

'Steady, man,' said Lowe curtly. 'What's the matter with your mistress?'

'She's dead, sir!' answered the servant tremulously. 'She's dead, and the bed's all over blood! Oh, my God!'

Lowe's eyes narrowed.

'Pull yourself together!' he said.

'I found her,' whispered Minter huskily. 'I was in the passage when Molly took in the tea. It was awful! Awful!' His breath came unevenly.

'Take me to Mrs. Hammond's room!' snapped the dramatist harshly.

The man was on the verge of hysteria and he deliberately made the order as stern as possible to bring him to his senses.

'Yes, s-sir,' stammered Minter.

He led the way dazedly along the

corridor, across the landing and into the opposite passage on which Mrs. Hammond's bedroom door opened. A frightened maid, her hands covering her face, was sobbing against the wall.

'In — in there, sir,' whispered Minter hoarsely.

'Take that girl away,' said Lowe, 'and let the cook or one of the other servants look after her. Then come back here.'

He crossed the threshold of the big bedroom, remembering as he did so his last interview with Mrs. Hammond. And then as he saw the bed he caught his breath.

The woman lay half in and half out, her head almost touching the floor. There was blood on her face and on the crumpled sheets, blood, too, on the carpet, and from her breast protruded the hilt of a knife. Clutched in her hand was something that gleamed whitely in the rays of the morning sun that streamed through the window.

Lowe, his face stern and set, went over and looked down at the dead woman. Here was the explanation for the midnight prowler. Here was the reason for that stealthy excursion through the dark and silent corridors of the sleeping house. Had the unknown already committed the crime when he had gone down to the lounge, or had this been perpetrated while Lowe had been unconscious? Perhaps the doctor's evidence would settle the question.

He peered at the white thing in Mrs. Hammond's hand and saw that it was a card. It seemed to be held loosely and he received confirmation of this when, taking it by the edge, he attempted to draw it out. It came easily, the half of a torn postcard. One side was blank. On the other was the crude drawing of the dangling man, and nothing else.

19

Inspector Cotter is Puzzled

Once more Backwaters was in the hands of the police. A burly constable stood in the hall, stolid, unimaginative, staring before him and apparently unconscious of the scared looks that were directed at him by the members of the household as they passed. In the upstairs bedroom the Divisional Surgeon was making his examination while the photographers waited impatiently in the corridor without.

Inspector Cotter, his face grave and worried, stood talking to Trevor Lowe. The dramatist had notified him of the tragedy at once, and Cotter had arrived post-haste. The rest of the household had been informed, and the inspector, while he waited for the arrival of the Divisional Surgeon, had questioned them all without, however, eliciting anything of importance.

They had apparently heard nothing

during the night. The shock, when they learned of Mrs. Hammond's death, had been a big one; Cavendish was horrified. Marjorie Lovelace, pale and frightened, answered the questions put to her like an automaton. John Moore looked as though he had been wakened from a bad dream and was not completely conscious. The cook was in hysterics and Minter went about with a dazed expression and a face that was still grey from the sight he had seen.

'This,' said Lowe in a low voice, 'rather upsets your theory, Cotter. There's no possible motive for Cavendish having committed this crime.'

The inspector looked dubious.

'There's certainly something in what you say, sir,' he admitted. 'At the same time he could have done it. He was in the house.'

'So were seven other people!' retorted the dramatist, 'if you include the servants. If you take my advice you'll hold up that warrant.'

'I had already decided to do so,' said Cotter. 'Still, I'm not altogether giving

Cavendish a clean bill. Was this person who attacked you a man, Mr. Lowe?'

The dramatist shook his head.

'That I can't tell you,' he answered. 'I never saw who did it. For all I know it might have been a woman, although I'm inclined to doubt it considering the force of the blow.'

'I don't know that that applies,' muttered Cotter. 'Women are pretty athletic these days, what with one thing and another.' He scratched his head. 'What do you make of that card?'

'I don't make anything of it,' declared Lowe, 'except that it links the murders with those anonymous letters. It was put in her hand after death, that's obvious. It was stuck in her fingers the same as you might stick it in a rack. She wasn't clutching it at all.'

'It's a queer business,' said the inspector, 'and I thought it was all plain and above-board.'

'Well, I told you,' said Lowe, 'that you were being too optimistic. There's depths here that we haven't started to fathom, I'm convinced of it. Cavendish and

Secket are side issues. I don't think they've got anything at all to do with the main motive.'

'What is the main motive?' growled Cotter. 'That's the question.'

'Yes, that is the question,' said the dramatist. 'When you've found that you've found everything. I'm not even sure in my own mind that the murder of Mrs. Hammond touches the main motive.'

Cotter's eyes were startled as he looked up quickly.

'What d'you mean by that?' he asked. 'You're not suggesting, surely, that the person who killed Mrs. Hammond isn't the same who killed her husband and Venita Shayne?'

'No. I'm not suggesting anything so ridiculous,' answered Lowe. 'But I'm inclined to believe that whereas the murder of Venita Shayne and Montague Hammond were premeditated, this one was not. I believe, if one could use such a phrase, that it was a murder of convenience, that Mrs. Hammond was killed because she knew too much — or guessed too much.'

Before Cotter could reply the Divisional

Surgeon approached them.

'Well,' he said. 'It's a messy business, but there's one thing, she didn't know much about it. In my opinion she died instantly.'

'The state of the bed,' said Cotter, 'looks as if there'd been a struggle.'

'Yes, it does,' said the doctor. 'But I don't think there was. The knife went straight into the heart, and although the appearance of the body and the disturbance of the bedclothes looks as if she'd made a fight for it, I don't think she knew anything about it.'

'Then how do you account for her appearance?' said the inspector.

The Divisional Surgeon shrugged his shoulders.

'I don't pretend to account for it,' he remarked. 'But if you want me to give an opinion I should say it was done after death to suggest that there had been a struggle — '

'Or,' interrupted Lowe, 'which, if you'll forgive me, doctor, is a more reasonable supposition, that the murderer was looking for something.'

'What?' demanded Cotter, and the dramatist smiled faintly.

'That I can't tell you. But it seems more reasonable to suppose that than to suppose that he would take the trouble to fake the appearance of a struggle.'

'Most probably you're right,' agreed the doctor.

'But what could he have been looking for?' muttered Cotter.

'That is impossible to conjecture,' said Lowe. 'And anyway, it's only a theory. Tell me, Doctor, I should imagine it would have been difficult for the killer to have escaped bloodstains with so much blood about?'

'You're quite right,' said the Divisional Surgeon. 'The blood must have spurted pretty badly when the knife was driven in.'

'In that case,' said the inspector quickly, 'there must be traces on the clothing.' He was at the door before the words had left his lips and calling for his sergeant. The man appeared. 'Search the whole house,' ordered Cotter, 'including everybody's luggage. You're looking for bloodstained clothing. Jump to it!'

The man obeyed, and the inspector came back with a satisfied smile.

'There's scarcely been time for the clothes to have been got rid of,' he said complacently. 'We might find a clue.'

Trevor Lowe was not so optimistic.

'You've forgotten the proximity of the river,' he remarked. 'A weighted bundle wouldn't take more than a minute or two to dispose of.'

Cotter's face fell.

'I'll have it dragged!' he snapped. 'Better let the photographers in now, eh?'

There was nothing more to be learned from the bedroom, both Lowe and Cotter had already made a careful search without discovering anything of importance, and leaving the room in the charge of the photographers they went downstairs, accompanied by the Divisional Surgeon. In the hall they met Eric Norman, his face anxious and troubled.

'Have you found anything?' he asked.

Lowe shook his head. The press agent clicked his teeth.

'My God, it's dreadful!' he said. 'Poor

Venita, then Hammond, now — this. What is behind it?'

'I'd give a lot to be able to answer your question,' said the dramatist gravely.

'It all seems so senseless,' muttered Norman. 'I can't see any reason for it.' He looked from one to the other hesitantly, and then went on: 'D'you think there'd be any objection to my going up to Town? I've got a business to attend to, you know, and — '

'That rests with Inspector Cotter,' answered Lowe.

The inspector was reluctant. At this stage of the proceedings it was obvious that he preferred to have all the members of the household where he knew where to find them.

'I'd much rather you didn't, sir,' he said.

'But look here,' argued Norman, 'it's most important that I should go to my office if only for an hour or so. There are certain things that I can only attend to personally. If you're under the impression that I had anything to do with it — '

'It isn't that, sir,' said Cotter interrupting him. 'I'm not saying that you had anything to do with it. But we don't know at present who had anything to do with it.'

'Well, I'm not likely to run away,' growled the press agent. 'I shouldn't get very far if I tried.'

'No, that's true, sir,' admitted the inspector. 'Well, if you'll promise to come back as soon as you've completed your business I don't mind stretching a point.'

'Thank you very much,' said Norman. 'I'll be back, at the latest, by six.' His expression was relieved, and with a nod he hurried away.

Cotter frowned dubiously.

'I suppose it'll be all right,' he muttered. 'You're coming up with me to see Miss Shayne's solicitors, aren't you, Mr. Lowe?'

'Yes,' said the dramatist. 'I think we may learn something there.'

'Well, it'll be a bit of a change if we learn something somewhere,' growled Cotter. 'This is the first murder case I've handled. The Chief Constable wanted to call in the Yard, but I persuaded him to let me have a try, though it looks as if I am going to fall down.'

'It's early to talk like that,' said the dramatist. 'You've only been on the case a few days, Cotter.'

'And I thought I had it all cut and dried,' said the inspector despondently. 'And now this comes and upsets all my calculations. Although,' he added, brightening a little, 'there's nothing to prove my original theory wasn't right.'

'No. But this fresh crime goes a long way towards vindicating Cavendish,' said the dramatist. 'Your theory at least gives him a possible motive for killing Venita Shayne and Hammond, but you can't suggest any practical reason why he should have killed Mrs. Hammond.'

'Can you suggest any reason why anyone should!' retorted the inspector.

'Yes,' said Lowe to his surprise. 'I can. Look at it this way. Suppose Mrs. Hammond knew something that was dangerous to the murderer's safety. Supposing he, or she, was aware of this and was also aware that Mrs. Hammond was going to speak. There's a reasonable motive.'

'Which,' said Inspector Cotter triumphantly, 'could also apply in the case of

Cavendish. Perhaps she remembered something that implicated him.'

'You're an obstinate fellow,' said Lowe with a slight smile. 'You don't intend to be prised loose from your pet theory without a struggle, do you?'

'It isn't that!' protested Cotter. 'But I can't see anyone else. Cavendish had the motive and the opportunity. Those are two perfectly strong arguments against him.'

'I'm perfectly willing to admit,' said the dramatist, 'that Cavendish is the star suspect. But that doesn't prove that he's guilty, and I, personally, don't think he is. However, it won't do any harm to hold your hand for a day or two.'

Cotter acquiesced in this. He had no wish to make a precipitate move, which might lead to a great deal of trouble. After all, Cavendish was the son of a wealthy and influential man, and an arrest without sufficient evidence to back it up would result in quite a lot of unpleasantness. There was always the possibility that the killer was no one they knew, a stranger who had gained access to the house from without.

Lowe did not believe this, neither did Cotter, but they had to take it into consideration.

The morning passed slowly. The sergeant whom the inspector had detailed to examine the rooms and belongings of the various people in the house reported failure. He had found nothing, no article of clothing whatsoever that bore any trace of bloodstains.

Just before lunch boats arrived, containing men who set about methodically dragging the river in the vicinity of the waterfront. They were still engaged on their fruitless task when Lowe and Cotter, leaving the house in charge of the sergeant and a constable, set off for London.

Venita Shayne's solicitors, Messrs. Abercrombie and Smith, occupied a large and prosperous looking office in Piccadilly. Mr. Reginald Abercrombie, a grey haired, extremely neat old gentleman, received them gravely.

'I needn't say,' he said, 'how shocked I was to learn of my client's tragic death. A terrible end to a life that was so promising.' He coughed dryly.

'You acted as legal adviser to Miss Shayne for some time, sir?' asked the inspector.

'For nearly three years,' replied the lawyer. 'Not so very long compared with some of our other clients, but long enough to feel profound regret at a loss which the entertainment world will find difficulty in replacing.'

Trevor Lowe shifted a little impatiently m his chair. He was not at all impressed by Mr. Abercrombie's rather stilted expressions of grief. They were not sincere. He felt that the lawyer considered that the occasion warranted something of the sort and produced it from a set formula, which he kept for such moments.

'You handled all Miss Shayne's affairs?' he inquired, and Mr. Abercrombie nodded.

'Yes,' he answered. 'With the exception, of course, of her contracts. They were handled by her agent.'

'Were you aware,' continued the dramatist, 'that she was married?'

The expression on the lawyer's face

answered his question before he put the answer into words.

'Married?' he echoed in surprise. 'No. I had not the least idea that Miss Shayne was married. When did this happen? Who was she married to?'

'It happened six years ago, and the man's name is Joe Secket,' said the dramatist. 'You'll probably be receiving a visit from him shortly.'

'Dear me,' said Mr. Abercrombie. 'Miss Shayne never mentioned this to me. I was under the impression that she was a spinster.'

'So was nearly everybody who knew her, I think,' said Lowe. 'I have only this man Secket's word, but I'm under the impression he was speaking the truth. He seemed prepared to back up his statement with the marriage certificate.'

'Very extraordinary!' muttered the lawyer. 'Very extraordinary indeed. The last time I saw Miss Shayne she hinted that she was shortly about to become engaged to the son of a very well known member of the nobility.'

'I'm aware of that,' said Lowe. 'In fact

she actually did become engaged.'

'But,' said Mr. Abercrombie, 'how could she if she was already married, as you say, to this man Secket.'

'I rather think Miss Shayne was prepared to forget that,' answered the dramatist, and the lawyer stared at him, frowning.

'You surely don't mean,' he said, 'that she would have carried this engagement to its natural conclusion? That she would have actually married this — er — man, whoever he was?'

'I think she would,' replied Lowe.

'But my dear sir!' Mr. Abercrombie waved a beautifully manicured hand. 'Do you realise that she would have been committing bigamy?'

'I do. But I don't think it would have troubled her in the slightest,' retorted the dramatist. 'I think Miss Shayne would have been prepared to have committed any crime to achieve her desires.'

'Really! Really!' Mr. Abercrombie's frown deepened. 'I feel you are being a little harsh. My client was a most honourable lady. I cannot allow such a suggestion to be made without protest.'

'So honourable,' said Lowe grimly 'that she only became engaged by blackmailing the person concerned!'

'Blackmailing!' Mr. Abercrombie infused such an expression of horror into his tone that Lowe concealed a smile. 'Good gracious me! Have you proof of this?'

'The proof,' said the dramatist quietly, 'is, I'm given to understand, in your office!'

20

The Deed-Box

Mr. Reginald Abercrombie surveyed him in amazement, an amazement that slowly changed to an expression of outraged dignity.

'Are you insinuating, sir,' he demanded softly, 'that I was a party to this alleged blackmail?'

'No! No!' said Lowe hastily. 'You misunderstand me, Mr. Abercrombie. What I meant was, that from information I have received, certain letters which Miss Shayne held over this man's head are deposited with your firm.'

The lawyer's face cleared.

'Oh, I see! I see!' he said. 'Yes, that is, of course, a possibility. Although I must have proof before I am prepared to believe this — er — charge which you bring against my unfortunate client.'

'I think,' said Lowe, 'if you examine the documents deposited in your care by

Miss Shayne you will receive all the proof you require.'

The lawyer pursed his lips, hesitated, and pressed a button on his desk. A clerk came in.

'Fetch me the deed-box labelled Shayne,' ordered Mr. Abercrombie, and the man departed. 'It is certainly true,' murmured the lawyer when the man had gone, 'that Miss Shayne used, from time to time, to deposit in our care certain documents of value. But I'm very loath to believe what you tell me.' He shook his head. 'Very loath indeed,' he added, as though to make the point perfectly clear to them.

'I can understand how you feel in the matter,' said Lowe. 'But I assure you that I am not making this charge without proof. By the way, did Miss Shayne make a will?'

'No, unfortunately,' replied the lawyer. 'I had been trying to persuade her to for some considerable time, but she kept putting it off. People do, you know. A very unwise proceeding.'

'Then,' said the dramatist, 'everything she possessed goes to this man Secket.'

'If he can provide satisfactory proof that a marriage took place between them,' said Mr. Abercrombie.

The clerk returned at that moment carrying a large black steel box, on the side of which was painted in white letters 'Venita Shayne'. He placed it silently on the desk in front of his employer and as silently took his departure.

'Was Miss Shayne well off?' asked Lowe, as Mr. Abercrombie deliberately produced a bunch of keys from his pocket and selected one.

'She was not rich in the accepted sense of the word,' replied the lawyer. 'She earned a lot of money, but her expenses were, naturally considering her position, very heavy. I don't know what her current balance is at the bank, but she had shares and securities approximating to — er — something in the nature of seven thousand pounds.'

Lowe thought of Joe Secket. This respectable amount would go to that unpleasant gentleman.

The lawyer unlocked the deed-box, opened it, and peered within.

'The bulk of the contents of this,' he remarked, 'are unknown to me. As you will see they have been enclosed in envelopes and marked, in the majority of cases, with initials. I must therefore disclaim all knowledge of what they contain.'

The dramatist's lips twitched. Mr. Abercrombie was a careful man. Much as he might apparently disbelieve the charges that had been brought against his dead client he was not taking any chances. By disclaiming all knowledge of the contents of the deed-box he dissociated himself from any unpleasant discoveries that might be made.

'It is a little irregular,' he said, 'for me to allow you access to these documents, but — er — in the circumstances I suppose — '

'I'll take all responsibility, sir,' put in Inspector Cotter, and the lawyer uttered a relieved sigh.

'In that case I am absolved,' he remarked. 'Perhaps we had better examine the contents together.' He was obviously bursting with curiosity.

A number of stout, manila envelopes,

some thin and some bulky, were removed from the box and placed on the desk. Trevor Lowe and the inspector drew up their chairs and the dramatist rapidly scanned the superscriptions. One marked H.C. he picked up, slit open the top, and shook out a number of letters. A glance and he saw that Harold Cavendish had spoken the truth.

'These concern the matter I referred to,' he said quietly, and passed two of the letters over to the lawyer.

Mr. Abercrombie scanned them with ever-increasing concern.

'Dear me,' he murmured, 'there seems to be no doubt. I am amazed and horrified.'

'You will, of course,' said the dramatist, 'treat this as entirely confidential?'

The lawyer stiffened.

'Everything that passes in this office, Mr. Lowe,' he replied with dignity, 'is confidential. Naturally I should not dream of mentioning the matter beyond these walls.'

'Let us see what the other envelopes contain,' said Lowe, and opened them one by one.

As he examined the contents his lips pursed and he whistled softly.

'Venita Shayne appears to have been much worse than we expected,' he remarked gravely. 'How any of these things came into her possession is a mystery. There's no doubt she was carrying on a very lucrative sideline of blackmail. Here's a confession signed by Secket concerning that theatre robbery he mentioned. She must have forced that out of him and held it over him, using the threat to ensure his silence concerning their marriage.'

They went through the rest carefully. For the most part they consisted of indiscreet letters, some written to Venita Shayne herself, some to other people, but all bearing the names of rich and influential men to whom a breath of scandal would have meant disaster.

Lowe was eagerly searching for something concerning Hammond, but in this he was disappointed. Among the whole box the producer was not mentioned.

'Anyway,' he remarked, 'I think we have sufficient evidence here to show what sort of a woman Miss Venita Shayne was.'

'I'm horrified!' said the lawyer. 'I had no idea. She was such a child-like, innocent-looking girl. To bring herself to — to —'

Lowe smiled.

'I think the childishness and the innocence were part of her stock-in-trade,' he said. 'She fooled most people.'

Inspector Cotter sighed wearily.

'Well, we know a little more than we did, but not much,' he declared. 'I suppose, as a matter of routine, we'll have to inquire among these people mentioned here and find out what they were doing at the time of her death. Any one of them had a motive for getting rid of the woman.'

'The trouble is,' said the dramatist, 'that although plenty of people had a motive for getting rid of Venita Shayne it doesn't follow they had a motive for killing Montague Hammond and Mrs. Hammond.'

'Good heavens!' exclaimed Mr. Abercrombie. 'You don't mean to say there's been another crime?'

'I'm afraid there has, sir,' said the inspector. 'Mrs. Hammond was killed during the night.'

The lawyer clicked his teeth.

'Dreadful! Dreadful!' he murmured. 'A shocking series of tragedies, Inspector Cotter!'

'Shocking enough, sir,' said the inspector grimly. 'What's that you've got hold of, Mr. Lowe?'

Trevor Lowe had come upon an envelope that he had not previously opened. It bore no superscription. Sliding his thumb under the flap he ripped it and withdrew the contents. It was a birth certificate, registered at Manchester, and certified the birth of a girl. The date was twenty-two years ago and the name of the baby was given as Marjorie Nita Hinkley. He looked at the names of the parents and raised his eyebrows.

'D'you remember that marriage certificate we found in Hammond's safe?' he inquired.

The inspector nodded.

'Yes,' he answered. 'What about it?'

'Well, here's a birth certificate of a

child born to Mr. and Mrs. Hinkley. It was born twenty-two years ago, which corresponds to the age Venita Shayne would be if she was still alive. I don't think there's any doubt that this is her birth certificate.'

'You mean that Shayne was not her real name?' said Cotter.

'Yes,' replied Lowe. 'I never imagined it was. Most stage people select professional names, and Venita Shayne always sounded to me too euphonious to be real. I think her name was Hinkley and she's the child of Mollie Dwyer and James Hinkley mentioned in the marriage certificate.'

'Well, who were they?' muttered the inspector. 'And why did Hammond keep that certificate?'

Lowe made no reply. A glimmer of an idea had occurred to him.

'If Venita Shayne changed her name James Hinkley could have done the same,' he murmured after a pause.

The inspector and the lawyer stared at him, frowning.

'I don't quite get you, Mr. Lowe,' said Cotter.

'It's only an idea of mine,' said Lowe. 'Listen. We know nothing about Montague Hammond prior to his sudden success. Even his lawyer couldn't take us back further than seventeen years.'

A light broke on the puzzled Cotter.

'You mean — ' he began.

'I mean,' said Trevor Lowe, 'that a man doesn't usually keep a marriage certificate that isn't his. I mean, or I'm suggesting, that Montague Hammond's real name was James Hinkley, and that prior to his marriage with Mrs. Hammond he was a widower, that his first wife was Mollie Dwyer.'

'Then,' said the inspector slowly, 'if that birth certificate refers to Venita Shayne she was Hammond's child.'

The dramatist nodded.

'Which accounts for his fondness for her,' he answered, 'and the fact that he left her half his money. It's got to be proved, but I think I'm right. Yes, I think Venita Shayne was Montague Hammond's daughter!'

21

Deadlock!

There was nothing more to be learned from Mr. Abercrombie, and very shortly after Lowe and Cotter took their leave. The inspector, after some little demur on the part of the lawyer, obtained permission to carry away with him the contents of the deed-box.

They went from the solicitor's office to the bank at which Venita Shayne had kept her account. The manager had been expecting them, but could offer no useful information. Their visit resulted in a complete blank. He had only met the dead woman once when she had come to open the account. That had been two years and six months ago. She had paid in a cheque of Mr. Montague Hammond's for the sum of three thousand pounds, and since then cheques for varying amounts had been received to be credited to her account fairly regularly.

Lowe asked to see the passbook and it was shown him, but none of the cheques bore the signatures that coincided with those of the deed-box. If Venita Shayne had extracted money from the various people over whom she had a hold she had done it very cleverly. The bulk of the cheques that had been paid into her account had been signed by Montague Hammond.

They went to Hammond's bank, but learnt nothing here, either. None of the dead producer's cheques, which he had paid from time to time into his credit, had any relation at all with the people whom Venita Shayne had evidently been blackmailing.

It had occurred to Lowe that she might have cashed cheques through Hammond, but this conjecture was evidently wrong.

'Well, there we are,' said Cotter rubbing his chin as they stood on the pavement, after this last visit. 'There's nothing else we can do.'

'I'm afraid there isn't,' agreed the dramatist, 'though the line of investigation seems fairly evident.'

'You mean,' said the inspector, 'to follow up this Hinkley clue?'

Lowe nodded.

'That's the obvious thing to do,' he answered. 'But it's going to take time, and I think it can best be left in your hands. Scotland Yard will help you.'

'While we're up here we may as well go and see them,' growled Cotter.

They drove to the embankment and presently were seated in the cheerless office of Detective-Inspector Shadgold. He was pleased to see Lowe and listened to the reason for their visit with interest.

'It's going to be a difficult job,' he said, 'but I'll do my best. I'll get on to it right away.'

And there for several days to come they were forced to leave it.

The inquest on Venita Shayne took place the following morning. It was a simple affair, consisting merely of the identification of the body and the medical evidence. Cotter asked for and was granted a fortnight's adjournment.

The inquest on Hammond had been

arranged to follow immediately, and the procedure in this case was exactly the same. When it was over Cotter interviewed the people who had been present at the time of the two crimes.

'There will be another inquest the day after tomorrow,' he announced, 'on Mrs. Hammond. I shall require everyone at the proceedings. In the meanwhile there is no reason why you should remain at Backwaters. I have your addresses and the subpoenas will reach you in the usual course of things. I must, however, warn you that no one must attempt to leave the country or the addresses which I have been given.'

There was relief on every face. The prospect of being allowed to leave the house on which the shadow of death rested so heavily was evidently welcome to everyone. It might have been less welcome, thought Lowe to himself, if they had known what he did, that each was to be subjected to a close watch, which Cotter had arranged for.

When the inspector had finished his short speech Lowe signalled to Marjorie

Lovelace and took her aside.

'I want to ask you a question, Miss Lovelace,' he said. 'When I first came down here during that tea-party if you remember on the loggia, you gave me the impression that you disliked Venita Shayne intensely. Was I right?'

The girl looked at him hesitantly.

'Yes, you were quite right Mr. Lowe,' she said in a low voice. 'I — I hated her!'

'Perhaps,' said the dramatist, 'you'd tell me why?'

'You'll probably think it's childish,' she answered, after a pause, 'but Venita Shayne once got me the sack. I was playing in one of Mr. Hammond's shows where, as usual, she was starred. My part was not a very large one, but it was showy, and I flatter myself that I played it well. In fact the notices that appeared after the first night were extraordinarily good. Every single one of them mentioned me and gave me an excellent report. I was naturally pleased, but Venita was furious. She hated anyone to get even a tiny bit of the limelight that she considered her exclusive right, and she insisted that Mr. Hammond should get somebody else. I know he was annoyed, I believe they had a row over it, at least I was told so by another member of the company. But anyway, she had her way as she usually did in the end, and I was fired. It was a mean thing to do because she knew that I was very hard-up at the time and that the job meant a lot.'

'I see. Well, I'm glad you told me,' said Lowe. 'I suppose you've no idea why Mrs. Hammond disliked her?'

'She disliked her because she was jealous,' answered the girl at once. 'Anybody could see that. She worshipped Monty, and she thought he was altogether too fond of Venita.'

'I think he was,' said the dramatist quietly, 'but not for the reason which most people imagined.'

Marjorie Lovelace looked at him quickly.

'What d'you mean?' she asked.

'I think,' said Lowe, skating round the truth without disclosing what he believed, 'that he was fond of her in a fatherly way.'

'Yes, I think you're right,' she answered. 'I, personally, never thought there was anything else in it, but of course Venita, with her usual pleasure in making other people unhappy, flaunted her power over him in front of Eva. She — it's not a nice thing to say — but she could be beastly at times.'

Harold Cavendish strolled out on to the lawn at that moment and joined them.

'I've been looking for you,' he said, addressing the girl. 'I've phoned the garage at Bray for a car to take me up to town. If you'd like to I'd be awfully pleased if you'd come with me.'

She flushed slightly.

'That's very nice of you, Mr. Cavendish,' she said. 'I should be delighted.'

'I'll be here in a quarter of an hour,' said the young man. 'Will that be too soon for you?'

She shook her head.

'No, I brought very little down,' she answered, 'so I haven't got much to pack. I'll be ready then.'

She left them and Cavendish turned to Lowe.

'Well,' he said, 'has anything been discovered?'

The dramatist shook his head.

'Nothing definite,' he replied. 'The police are still conducting inquiries, of course.'

Cavendish made a grimace.

'The thing that surprises me,' he remarked, 'is that I'm still at large. I fully expected, after the information I gave you, to be arrested.'

'The reason that you're not,' answered Lowe, 'is this third crime. If someone hadn't killed Mrs. Hammond that night I think you'd find yourself in the local lock-up.'

'It wouldn't have surprised me,' declared the other. 'I wonder what's at the back of it all? I never met Mrs. Hammond, of course, but it was a dreadful thing!'

'The whole affair is dreadful,' said Lowe gravely. 'And at the present moment there's no vestige of a solution.'

Cavendish took a sheet of paper from his pocket and scribbled on it.

'I wish you'd let me know, Mr. Lowe,' he said seriously, 'if anything comes to light, or if I can help in any way. This is my address and it'll always find me.' He handed the paper to Lowe, and the dramatist, after a glance at it, stowed it away in his pocket.

As he did so Inspector Cotter came out on to the loggia and called to him. With a word of farewell to Cavendish Lowe went to see what he wanted.

'There's a telephone call for you,' said Cotter. 'They're holding on.'

Lowe made his way rapidly to the study and picked up the receiver. Arnold White's voice came over the wire.

'Hello!' said the secretary, 'I've been trying to get you before, but they said you were out. I followed that fellow. He went straight from here to Camden Town to a house in Rice Street. After a little while he came out again and took a bus to the West End where he spent the evening in several pubs. By the time he'd finished he was a bit under the weather, but he only went home again. I got hold of Burke and he's taking it in turns with me to keep an eye on the house. Was that right?'

'Quite right,' said Lowe. 'So he does live in Rice Street?'

'Oh, yes, he lives there all right,' answered Arnold. 'I made one or two inquiries in the shops in the district, and they know him well.'

'Continue to keep an eye on him,' said his employer. 'I shall be coming up to Town later today. I'll see you at the flat.' He rang off and went down to the lounge.

'By the way,' he said to Cotter when he had recounted the gist of White's conversation, 'I suppose you're leaving somebody in charge here.'

'Sergeant Winter,' said Cotter. 'I'm leaving him until further notice.'

Marjorie Lovelace and Harold Cavendish departed a few moments later and were followed shortly after by John Moore and Eric Norman. When Cotter himself had gone Lowe sought out Minter.

'You'll be staying on here, I suppose,' he said, 'until the solicitors have decided what is going to happen to the place?'

'Yes, sir,' answered the servant. He smiled ruefully. 'I shall be about the only one, with the exception of the sergeant,' he added. 'The cook and the maid are leaving. They refuse to sleep here now everybody's cleared out.'

'They can scarcely be blamed,' murmured the dramatist. 'I shall be going myself shortly.'

He slipped a pound note into the man's hand and went upstairs to pack. At two o'clock he left Backwaters and drove up to London, arriving at Portland Place just before four.

White was still out, probably on the job of watching Mr. Secket, but his housekeeper welcomed him and bustled about to get him some tea. The familiar study looked cosy and pleasant, and weary from the events of the last few days Lowe settled himself in his favourite armchair with a sigh of content.

There was nothing much he could do now until the police had succeeded in tracing James Hinkley and either proving or disproving his theory that he and Montague Hammond had been one and the same. He was convinced that if this was so and Venita Shayne had been Hammond's daughter something in their past provided the motive for the murders.

Never in his wildest imaginings did

he dream of what was to come to light, or how the knowledge that he was to acquire within the next few days was to make the mystery still deeper.

22

Hinks

The detectives employed by Inspector Cotter to watch the movements of the various people concerned in the 'Backwaters Mystery' as Frank Littlewood of the *Echo* named it, went about their jobs conscientiously, but without results. The watch, which Arnold White and Burke, a retired detective whom Lowe occasionally employed for such purposes, divided between them on Mr. Secket was equally devoid of incident. The man had visited Messrs. Abercrombie and Smith and proved beyond reasonable doubt that he and Venita Shayne had married, as he had stated.

Lowe learned this from Mr. Abercrombie himself when he telephoned the lawyer and put the question.

Backwaters, deserted, except for the sergeant and Minter, lay silent and closed and was likely to remain so for a considerable time. Hammond's property, now that his wife was dead, belonged to no one. There was no next of kin so far as was known, and unless someone came forward claiming relationship it was likely to go to the State. The house, in the opinion of Mr. Harrison Peek, looked like proving more of a liability than an asset, for it was doubtful, after what had occurred there, if anyone would buy it.

Lowe had one or two telephone conversations with Inspector Cotter, and during one of these learned that Harold Cavendish and Marjorie Lovelace seemed to have struck up a close friendship. He was not surprised, for the mutual attraction between them had been evident even during the early days of their meeting.

The mystery surrounding the deaths of Venita Shayne, Montague Hammond and his wife still occupied the greater part of the dramatist's thoughts. But he realised that patience was necessary, and during the ensuing days that passed without further word in connection with the affair, he occupied himself with various matters, though the strange series of crimes was never really out of his mind.

In order to clarify the situation he (as he usually did in an intricate case) jotted down the sequence of events together with any comments that occurred to him. And on the morning of the day that Shadgold arrived with his astounding news he read this over to refresh his memory.

Montague Hammond had for some time received a number of anonymous letters, couched in abusive and threatening terms, and signed with the drawing of a man hanging from a gallows.

Query. What lies behind this symbol?

He had also on several occasions become aware of somebody watching him and following him about.

Query. Was this person the writer of the anonymous letters?

Hammond had obviously been keeping something back.

Note. Probably aware of the meaning

of the symbol and the identity of the anonymous letter writer, and also the watcher. Seemed to be scared. Invited me down to Backwaters on excuse of discussing anonymous letter business, but really, in my opinion, because of this fear.

Venita Shayne arrives. Announces her forthcoming engagement to Harold Cavendish. On the following day is found strangled in Hammond's study with burn on right forearm caused by concentrated sun's rays through water-bottle, proving that crime was committed earlier than at first believed. This alters alibis.

Query. Was this done for a definite purpose by the murderer or just to confuse the issues?

Following morning Hammond on point of disclosing further information is killed by shot from island. Cavendish discovered on island admits has been there since previous day and interviewed Venita Shayne on lawn of Backwaters at two o'clock on the Saturday morning. Girl was not there because she expected to see him. She didn't know he was in the vicinity.

Query. What was Venita Shayne doing

237

at two o'clock in the morning waiting on the lawn?

Cavendish further admits hated Venita since she had blackmailed him into engagement because of certain letters she held concerning himself and another which, made public, would have produced a scandal, Venita Shayne's diary stolen from flat.

Query. Who by, and for what reason?

Among Hammond's effects marriage certificate found, between Mollie Dwyer and James Hinkley.

Query. Is James Hinkley Hammond's real name?

Man named Joe Secket claims to have married Venita Shayne six years previously, and, although refuses to admit the fact, was in the vicinity of Backwaters prior to, and possibly during, the time of the crime.

Query. Was this the man whom Shayne expected to meet at two o'clock when she was waiting on lawn at Backwaters?

Noises during the night lead to investigation and discovery of someone in lounge with candle.

Query. Who was this, and for what reason was the visit made to the lounge?

Attack on me obviously made to avoid discovery. Later Mrs. Hammond discovered murdered in her bed with card in her hand bearing drawing of gallows man. Indication that killer searched for something after committing crime. Doors and window latched and bolted. Therefore crime committed probably by member of household.

Query. Who?

General Remark. Who wrote the anonymous letters to Hammond and myself, and why? What significance is there in the signature drawing? Why was Hammond afraid? What is the motive behind the killing of Venita Shayne, the killing of Hammond, and the killing of Mrs. Hammond? Is it *one* motive, or have we to deal with separate motives?

Note. Am of the opinion that the motive for the first two murders is the same, but that Mrs. Hammond killed because she either suspected or knew something dangerous to murderer. Was Shayne Hammond's daughter?

He read through this summary of fact and conjecture and pursed his lips. It was a tough knot, a difficult problem. Difficult to search out the essentials.

He was still studying it when a knocking resounded through the flat and presently a familiar voice sounded in the hall. A moment later the maid ushered Shadgold into the study.

'Hello, Mr. Lowe!' grunted the Inspector, pushing his bowler hat to the back of his head and mopping his perspiring face. 'I've got some news for you. The report's already gone to Cotter, but I thought I'd come round and give you the result of the inquiries myself.'

'Which means,' murmured the dramatist, 'that you've been successful.'

'Yes, to a certain extent we have,' admitted Shadgold. 'We've succeeded in establishing the fact that Montague Hammond and James Hinkley were one and the same. You were right there. We got hold of a photograph, had duplicates made, and distributed throughout the country. The majority of the reports that came in were negative, but eventually we got a line and followed it up. Mollie Dwyer was a parlour maid in the house of a man called Langley. Hinkley married her at the Bloomsbury Registrar's Office. All that you know. The baby, a girl, was born in Manchester during the time Hinkley was appearing in a drama called *The World for Love*. What you don't know and what I've come round to tell you is who James Hinkley was. We've found that out, and it gave me a bit of a shock, I can assure you!'

'Well, who was James Hinkley?' said Lowe, his eyes gleaming.

'Ever heard of Hinks?' said Shadgold, and the dramatist uttered a startled exclamation.

'Hinks!' he breathed. 'Good God! You don't mean — you don't mean the *Public Executioner*?'

'He *was* the Public Executioner,' said the inspector. 'He died ten years ago. James Hinkley, alias Montague Hammond, was his son!'

23

The Shadow of the Gallows

It was not often that Shadgold had the satisfaction of surprising his friend, but this time he had succeeded with a vengeance. The dramatist stared at him, his lips parted and his eyes wide.

'Good Heavens!' he exclaimed when he had sufficiently recovered from the shock to be able to speak at all. 'Are you sure of this? There's no mistake?'

'Oh no, there's no mistake!' declared Shadgold complacently. 'That's who Montague Hammond was, the son of Hinks the Hangman.'

'It's incredible!' murmured Lowe.

'Incredible or not, it's the truth!' retorted the Inspector. 'I've got all the details at the Yard. Hinks was a Lancashire man. He was born just outside Manchester. His business was a cobbler, the same as his father's before him. He became Public

242

Executioner in nineteen hundred and nine. He was married and there were two sons. One died in the war and the other changed his name to James Hinkley and became an actor. That's your man, Hammond.'

Lowe's brows were furrowed. He was thinking rapidly. The signature to the anonymous letters, the little drawing, the man dangling from a gallows. Here was a connection. If Hammond's father had been the Public Executioner Hammond had recognised the connection. That's why he had been loath to court publicity by taking the matter to the police; had been loath to reveal that he was the son of Hinks the Hangman. But who had sent those letters?

Here was a fresh complication, which only seemed to make things more difficult. It offered an explanation for the drawings, but failed to throw any light on the rest of the affair. Who was this anonymous letter writer who chose as his signature a drawing that would remind the recipient that he was the son of the Public Executioner? And why had he chosen to remind him?

Vaguely the dramatist sensed something horrible. Behind this triple murder was something sinister and unpleasant, something that caused him to shiver inwardly.

'Well, I must congratulate you on a smart piece of work, Shadgold,' he said. 'It must have been a difficult job.'

'It was,' said the Inspector ruefully. 'But when it comes to that kind of work you can't beat our organisation.'

'What's known about Hinks?' asked the dramatist, beginning to pace slowly up and down.

'Very little,' said Shadgold. 'He carried out his job all right, although he did eventually die from drink.'

'Oh, he died from drink?' said Lowe. 'Ten years ago you said.'

'Roughly,' answered the inspector. 'I wouldn't be certain to a month or two, but I can easily find out if you think it's important.'

'I think everything's important,' said Lowe. 'We've only touched the fringe of the matter at the moment. I want to know all you can discover about Hinks and all you can discover about his sons — the whole family in fact. Who was his wife?'

'A Lancashire mill girl,' said Shadgold. 'I can tell you that now,'

'Find out everything you can about them,' urged Lowe. 'Particularly let me have a list of the murderers whom Hinks executed.'

The Scotland Yard man looked at him curiously.

'D'you think this is a crime of vengeance?' he said dubiously.

'I don't know what it is!' declared his friend. 'But I'm going to discover why. If it takes me ten years I'll find out! It's a most interesting problem, Shadgold. One of the most interesting I've ever come in contact with. Venita Shayne was Hammond's daughter. Mrs. Hammond was Hammond's wife. It looks to me as if someone was out to, and has succeeded in, killing the whole family. The whole family of Hinks the Hangman! What are you smiling at?'

For Shadgold's broad face had suddenly twisted into a grin.

'Hinks the Hangman,' replied the inspector. 'The way you put it sounded like that old game I used to play when I was a kid. You know: Binks the Butcher.'

Lowe smiled, too.

'Yes, I suppose it did,' he remarked, and became instantly grave again. 'There's nothing funny about this, Shadgold, nothing funny at all. We've got three dead people to prove that. It's a nasty business and I'd very much like to know the 'Why' of it? Crimes of vengeance are rare. I'm inclined to discount that until I've tried everything else. It's too far-fetched to suppose that anyone, say a relation, for argument's sake, of somebody who, in the course of his duty, Hinks hanged, should go to the length of wiping out his son, his grand-daughter, and his daughter-in-law purely out of vengeance. It doesn't sound feasible.'

'Unless the killer's a lunatic,' suggested the inspector. 'There's no accounting for what a madman 'ull do.'

'The killer here isn't mad!' declared Lowe. 'There's no sign of insanity about the crimes. They were cleverly planned and cleverly carried out.'

'Well, I don't know that I've helped you much,' said the Scotland Yard man. 'I'll certainly get on to Hinks and find out all that's known about him. Perhaps there'll be something that'll give you a clue, though I'm hanged if I know what!'

'Neither do I,' said Lowe. 'But that's all we can do. One thing we do know, the signature on those anonymous letters that Hammond received and I received and the drawing on the card that was found in Mrs. Hammond's hand definitely indicate that the person knew who Hammond was. It couldn't possibly be a coincidence. Therefore the motive has something to do with Hammond's relationship with Hinks.'

Shadgold shrugged his shoulders.

'That doesn't get you very far,' he remarked.

'No, but it gives us a basis on which to work,' said Lowe. 'No wonder Hammond changed his name. No wonder he was reluctant to take me fully into his confidence. He must have been practically born in the shadow of the gallows. I wonder what his business associates and friends would have thought, if they'd known who he was?'

'Personally,' said the practical Shadgold,

'I don't see why anybody should have minded. After all, the Public Executioner is an official of the State the same as a judge or a magistrate or a police officer. Somebody's got to do his job. There's nothing to be ashamed of in it.'

'No, but the majority of people don't look at it like that,' said the dramatist. 'They'd regard a relation of the hangman with horror and shrink away from him. Hammond knew that and — ' He paused. 'I wonder if Venita Shayne knew it?' he murmured thoughtfully.

'What difference does it make if she did?' demanded the inspector.

'It makes this difference,' said his friend. 'Mrs. Hammond once told me that her husband was afraid of Venita Shayne. If he knew of his relationship she may have held it over his head.'

'But she was his daughter!' protested the inspector. 'If she'd made it public it would have affected her, too.'

'Yes. But she may not have had any intention of making it public,' said Lowe. 'She may have merely used the knowledge as a threat. Hammond may not have been aware that she was bluffing.'

'Well,' said Shadgold, 'I don't know sufficient about the case to argue. But I wish you luck, Mr. Lowe.' He glanced at the clock. 'Now I must be off. I've got a conference in twenty minutes.'

He shook hands with his friend and the dramatist heard him go clumping across the hall. Lighting his pipe he sat down to think over the fresh item of information that had come his way.

Somehow, in Hammond's relationship to the dead hangman lay the motive behind the three murders. Of this he was convinced, but what was it? The major motives for murder are gain, jealousy and vengeance. Which of these applied in this instance? At first glance it seemed possible to eliminate gain and jealousy, but was it? Was his knowledge sufficient to warrant it? It was not! So far as was known there seemed to be no one who benefited by these three deaths. But it couldn't be taken as a definite fact, and there was no denying a considerable sum of money was involved.

Mr. Harrison Peek had stated that

there were no relations of the dead producer alive, but since he had not been aware of Hammond's real identity this statement had to be taken for what it was worth, which, in the light of what was now known, was nothing.

Shadgold had mentioned a brother who had died in the war, and it was quite feasible to suppose that this man might have had children who, in the present circumstances, would be Hammond's heirs. Was this the motive? Was it some unknown relative of Hammond's who had killed off the people who stood in the way of a fortune?

It was not an improbable suggestion, but it didn't explain the trimmings, the anonymous letters, the mysterious watcher, the theft of Venita's diary and the rest.

The difficulty with the whole business was that it was so involved, so many ramifications and unexplained odds and ends. If it were possible to discard the non-essentials it might be easier to see daylight. The trouble was to decide which were non-essentials and which were not.

The telephone bell rang in the midst of

his thoughts and he picked up the instrument a little impatiently.

'Hello!' he called. 'This is Trevor Lowe speaking.'

'This is Harrison Peek,' said the voice of the lawyer over the wire. 'Have you half an hour to spare, Mr. Lowe? I've had a communication from a firm of inquiry agents which I think settles a point you mentioned to me at Backwaters.'

'What's that?' asked the dramatist interestedly.

'You remember telling me Mr. Hammond informed you he had been watched? Well, those people state they were engaged to keep Mr. Hammond under observation.'

'By whom?' demanded Lowe as he paused.

'By Mrs. Hammond!' said the lawyer.

24

The Inquiry Agency

Trevor Lowe hung up the receiver with a little frown. Here was an unexpected explanation for the man whom Montague Hammond had said he had surprised on various occasions trailing him. And yet it was such a simple one that the dramatist wondered why he hadn't thought of it before. Mrs. Hammond had been furiously jealous of her husband, and since, without a doubt, rumour had coupled his name with Venita Shayne it was not surprising that she had taken this means to satisfy her suspicions.

He took a taxi to the offices of Messrs. Crandal and Peek and found Mr. Peek awaiting him.

'I thought I'd better let you know,' said the lawyer, 'since you raised the point when I saw you at Backwaters. These people appear to have learned of Mrs.

Hammond's death and forwarded us an account. Here it is.' He selected a document from several that lay before him and passed it over to the dramatist.

He scanned it rapidly. It was a fairly stiff account, and with it was a covering letter briefly stating that it had been incurred by Mrs. Hammond for watching and reporting on the movements of her husband. The agency was quite well known. It was run by a retired Scotland Yard inspector, a man called Hutchings, quite a legitimate and respectable concern.

'We shall, of course, settle the account from the estate,' said Mr. Peek. 'This, however, explains what Mr. Hammond meant when he told you of the strange man whom he had seen following him about.'

Lowe nodded.

'I'll go round and see these people,' he said. 'I'm much obliged to you for the information, Mr. Peek.'

He left the lawyer's offices and drove to the address of the agency, an office in Holborn. Ex-detective Inspector Hutchings received him at once.

'Come in, Mr. Lowe,' he said as the dramatist was ushered into the comfortably furnished inner room. 'What can I do for you, sir?'

'You can give me a little information,' said Lowe. 'I understand you were engaged by Mrs. Montague Hammond to watch her husband.'

The broad face of the man before him expressed surprise.

'Yes, that's perfectly true,' he answered. 'How did you know anything about it?'

'I'm looking into the matter of the murders,' explained Lowe. 'When your account reached Messrs. Crandal and Peek, Mr. Peek immediately 'phoned me.'

'Oh, yes. We sent in the account directly we heard of Mrs. Hammond's death,' said the inquiry agent. "Queer business, that. What's at the back of it?'

'That's what I'm doing my best to find out,' said Lowe. 'At the present moment I don't know. Tell me about this commission the dead woman gave you.'

'Well, it was a very ordinary one,' said the big man, leaning back in his chair. 'She arranged an appointment with me, came and saw me, and said she wanted her husband kept under observation. She was under the impression that he was spending a lot of his time with another woman and she wanted to make sure. It was the usual thing.' He shrugged his shoulders. 'I asked her if she was considering divorce proceedings and she said no. She merely wanted the information for her own satisfaction. We arranged terms, and I put one of my best men on the job. Periodically we forwarded reports to the lady and that was all. She had good reason for her suspicions, though,' he added. 'Hammond spent a great deal of his time at a flat in Weymouth Street belonging to this girl who was killed, Venita Shayne.'

'Which is not surprising,' said Lowe. 'considering that she happened to be his daughter.'

Hutchings whistled softly.

'Oh, she was his daughter, was she?' he said. 'By an earlier marriage, I suppose?'

The dramatist nodded.

'H'm!' commented the inquiry agent. 'Well, Mrs. Hammond had no idea of that.'

'No, she was unaware of the fact,' answered Lowe. 'I don't think that she even knew that her husband had been married before.'

'Why on earth didn't he tell her?' grunted Hutchings. 'Naturally his actions were liable to be misconstrued. When my man reported to me I naturally concluded that it was the usual business.'

'I think that was the general opinion amongst the circle in which he moved,' said the dramatist. 'And why he didn't explain the truth of the matter is beyond me. However, he didn't, and it was only quite accidentally that I discovered it.'

'It was stupid of him,' said the big man. 'Naturally his wife jumped to the worst conclusions. I suppose,' he added a little anxiously, 'there'll be no trouble over my account? We had nothing in writing and — '

'I don't think you need worry about that,' said Lowe. 'As a matter of fact Mr. Peek told me just now that he was settling it.'

He took his leave and came out into Holborn with a thoughtful expression on his face. One of the queer points in this strange affair had been satisfactorily cleared up. The watcher could now be eliminated from any participation in the murders. That was something achieved. If he could find a solution to some of the other incidents the confusion which surrounded the main issue might be tidied up.

He came to a decision, hailed a taxi, and instructed the driver to go to Rice Street.

It was a narrow turning off the Camden Road and the house occupied by Mr. Secket was a third of the way down on the right, an unpretentious building of old-fashioned stucco. As he dismissed the cab he saw White dawdling on the opposite side of the street. He gave no sign of recognition, and mounting the steps rang the bell.

An elderly, grey-haired woman, with tired eyes, answered his summons.

'Yes, sir, I think he's in,' she said in reply to his question. 'What name shall I tell him?'

Lowe gave her his card and she

disappeared up a narrow flight of dingily carpeted stairs. He heard a murmur of voices and then she returned.

'Will you come up, sir?' she called from halfway down the stairs, and he followed her up to the landing above.

Mr. Secket occupied a room facing the street, a shabbily furnished apartment, the principal furniture of which consisted of a bed, a table, and a rather lumpy looking chair. He eyed the visitor doubtfully as the landlady ushered him in and withdrew.

'What d'yer want to see me about?' he demanded.

'I thought I'd like a little chat, Mr. Secket,' said the dramatist pleasantly. 'I understand that you've taken my advice and been to Messrs. Abercrombie and Smith.'

'That's right,' grunted Secket. 'What about it?'

'There's nothing about it,' said Lowe. 'I think it was a wise move.'

'Well, it isn't any business of yours, anyway,' said Mr. Secket rudely. 'What've you come 'ere for?'

'I thought,' explained the dramatist, 'that you might be able to give me some information. On the Friday prior to your wife's death you received an anonymous letter, didn't you?'

Mr. Secket's head jerked up.

'Eh?' he exclaimed. 'How did you know that?'

'It's immaterial,' said Lowe sharply. 'The letter was signed with the drawing of a man dangling from a gallows. Now, what did it say?'

It was some time before he received a reply. Mr. Secket was obviously considering.

'I dunno why I shouldn't tell you,' he answered presently. 'I'd 'ave told you before when I was down at Backwaters only I didn't want to mix meself up with no trouble.' He went over to a chest of drawers, pulled one open, rummaged among its contents, and came back with a sheet of paper. 'There y'are! Read that!' he said.

It was in roughly printed characters, like the rest of the letters that Lowe had seen.

'*Your wife's plotting to double-cross you. Watch out or you'll find yourself in trouble.*'

The familiar drawing of the dangling man completed the message.

'When did you get this?' asked Lowe.

'On the Friday mornin',' answered Secket sullenly.

'D'you know who sent it?'

The man shook his head.

'No. I couldn't make it out,' he declared. 'Nobody knew Nita and I was married, you see. I thought at first p'raps maybe she was playin' some trick.'

'What made you think that?' asked the dramatist. 'She'd hardly warn you against herself.'

'You never knew with Nita,' grunted Mr. Secket. 'It might 'ave been part of some trick she was up to.'

'What did you do about it?' said Lowe.

'I didn't do anythin',' answered Secket quickly. 'I just took no notice of it.'

'When did you last see your wife?' said the dramatist suddenly, after a little pause.

'When did I last see 'er?' Mr. Secket

moistened his lips. 'Some time durin' the early part of last week,' he replied reluctantly. 'I can't remember when.'

'Now listen here, Secket,' said Lowe sternly. 'And listen carefully. Did you or did you not come down to Backwaters on Friday, the Friday before your wife was killed, and meet her at two o'clock in the morning on the lawn?'

'No I didn't!' cried Secket. 'And you can't prove I did! I didn't do nothin' of the sort!' His whole appearance belied his statement. The vehemence in his denial was overdone.

Lowe was certain he had hit the nail on the head.

'You *did* go to Backwaters!' he accused. 'You got this letter in the morning and you went down to tackle your wife about it. Now why not come across? I'm not the police. I don't even suspect you had anything to do with her death. I just want the truth, and I'm going to have it! If you don't tell me willingly I'll set the police to inquire into your movements and it shouldn't be difficult to trace them.'

Mr. Secket was plainly scared.

261

'Well, supposin' I did?' he mumbled. 'There's no harm in it, is there? I didn't stop. I came back again. I can prove that,' he added quickly, ''cause I got a friend who runs a garage to drive me down and bring me back.'

'Why couldn't you have said that before?' demanded the dramatist.

'Well,' Mr. Secket, now that he had decided to become confidential, made a great show of frankness. 'Well, to tell you the truth, mister, I didn't want to be mixed up in it. You see it was like this. I got that note and I couldn't make 'ead nor tail of it. I thought it was quite likely that Nita was up to somethin' or other and it worried me. I knew she was goin' down to Backwaters for the weekend so I telephoned at 'er flat and asked if I could see 'er. She said no, she was too busy, and I said it was urgent and couldn't I see 'er somewhere at 'Ammond's. I could tell by 'er voice this didn't please 'er. She didn't want me anywhere near 'er 'igh class friends. I said well what about meetin' me near the 'ouse after everybody 'ad gone to bed. At first she wouldn't 'ear of it until I threatened that if she didn't see me I'd come and knock at the door and demand to see 'er. Then she said all right, she'd be on the lawn about half-past one, and she'd let me in the side gate. Well, I got this feller I told you about to drive me down and she let me in. I showed 'er that note and she said it was all a lot of nonsense. She didn't know anythin' about it One thing and another led to words and we 'ad a bit of a row — '

'During which,' put in Lowe, 'you seized her by the wrist.'

Mr. Secket gaped at him.

' 'Ow d'you know that?' he said. 'You weren't there, was yer?'

'Never mind how I know,' said the dramatist impatiently. 'You did, didn't you?'

'Yes, I did,' admitted the man. 'But I didn't 'urt 'er although she gave me a proper tellin' off. That's all there is to it. I left and came back.'

'And came down again on the Saturday in the hope of renewing your quarrel?'

It was a shot in the dark and Lowe had no basis for making the statement, but his instinct told him it was the likely thing a man of Secket's type would do.

'Well, yes, I did,' the man admitted. 'But I never saw 'er. I 'ung about most of the day in the 'opes she might come out. I tell yer I was worried. I didn't know what she might be up to. She'd threatened all sorts of things over and over again. And then I 'eard what 'ad 'appened — ' He broke off.

'You mean,' said Lowe, 'you heard she'd been murdered?'

Secket nodded.

'Yes, and I was properly scared,' he answered. 'I went back to London as quick as I could, wonderin' whether I might be seen and whether I might be implicated.'

'It would have saved a lot of trouble,' said the dramatist, 'if you'd told Inspector Cotter and me this at first.'

'I didn't see 'ow it could 'elp matters,' said Mr. Secket. 'I 'ad nothin' to do with the killin', neither do I know who 'ad. I might 'ave got meself in a nasty jam by admittin' I was there, and that's all.'

Lowe frowned. The reason for Venita

Shayne's presence at two o'clock on that Saturday morning had been explained. But it didn't carry him very far. That Secket had anything to do with the murders he did not believe, but he could quite understand the little man's reluctance to admit he was in the vicinity at the time of the crime.

Without possessing a great deal of intelligence, he was shrewd enough to realise that he might be suspected, considering how much he derived from his wife's death.

The subsidiary details that were so puzzling were slowly being cleared up. He knew now who the watcher had been and also why Venita had been on the lawn at two o'clock. There still remained several other unexplained incidents. The robbery at the flat and the theft of the diary, and —

He broke off in his thoughts as an idea struck him.

'What did you do when you got back?' he said suddenly. 'You didn't pay a visit to Miss Shayne's flat, by any chance, did you?'

'Blimey, you've got second sight!' said Mr. Secket. ' 'Ow did you know that?'

'So you did, eh?' said the dramatist. 'Why? Was it you who took that diary?'

'Diary?' The man shook his head. 'No, I didn't take no diary. And there's nothin' against the law in a feller visitin' 'is wife's flat. You can't 'ave me on that.'

'I'm not trying to have you on anything,' said Lowe. 'I'm merely trying to get you to tell me the truth. You went to your wife's flat late on the Saturday night, admitting yourself by way of the fire-escape and the back door, the key of which you'd taken previously. Is that right?'

'That's right,' said Mr. Secket. 'Though 'ow you know beats me.'

'When did you take that key?' went on the dramatist. 'The maid, Stokes, remembers seeing it on the Friday when she cleaned down the dresser.'

'I took it on the Saturday evenin',' said Mr. Secket. 'I 'adn't no intention of doin' so. It was accidental as you might say. When I got back after 'earin' about Nita's death I got worryin', wonderin' whether there was anythin' at 'er flat which the perlice might find that 'ud look bad fer me. I don't want you to go thinkin' things,' he added hastily, 'but she might 'ave written down a lot o' lies — '

'In fact,' put in Lowe, 'you were looking for the confession which she forced you to sign concerning the theatre robbery. Is that it?'

'T'ain't much good me tellin' you anythin',' said Mr. Secket. 'You know it all. 'Ow did you know about that?'

'I've seen it. She'd deposited it with some other documents at her solicitors.'

'Sort of thing she would do,' said Mr. Secket savagely. 'Not that it means anythin'. I wrote it just to please her.'

'I'm sure you did,' said Lowe dryly. 'However, I'm not concerned with that. How did you get this key?'

'Well, I was tellin' yer,' said Mr. Secket. 'I 'opped along to Weymouth Street durin' the evenin' and was comin' up in the lift when I saw that woman Stokes — and a sour piece of goods she is! — goin' down the stairs. I didn't stop, I went on, and when I reached the front door of the flat it was ajar. I guessed then that she'd gone down to see a friend of 'ers on the next floor. 'Ere's me opportunity, I thought. I'd been goin' to ask 'er to let me 'ave a look round, not that I 'ad much 'opes she would. But 'ere was a chance I 'adn't reckoned on. I popped in, pinched the key, and slipped out before she came back.'

'And you didn't take the diary?' said Lowe.

''Ow could I?' said Mr. Secket. 'Venita 'ad it with 'er!'

'How do you know that?' snapped the dramatist.

'Because she told me on the Friday,' said Mr. Secket. 'She was in one of 'er cold furies, and she said, just afore I went: 'I'll 'ave a nice little bit to write in my diary before I go to bed, Joe.'

Lowe eyed the man keenly and came to the conclusion that he was speaking the truth. Venita Shayne's diary had been stolen at Backwaters. By whom, and for what reason?

25

The Slip

On the evening of the following day, true to his promise, Shadgold sent round a bulky envelope containing all that was known of the deceased Hinks.

Lowe read the information that the Scotland Yard man had hastily collected, and although it was interesting came to the conclusion when he had finished that it helped him very little.

The dead man had two sons, James and John. John had married a girl in his home town, the daughter of a grocer, who had died in giving birth to a child which had only survived its mother by six weeks. The marriage had taken place in the year before the war, and John Hinks had then been twenty-two. He had joined the Army towards the end of nineteen-fourteen, and had been reported missing in nineteen-sixteen.

No trace of him had afterwards been found. If this man was still alive — Lowe made a rapid calculation — he would be approximately forty-five.

James Hinks, otherwise Hinkley, otherwise Hammond, was the elder by nearly ten years. He had left home at the age of eighteen and nobody seemed to know very much what had happened to him.

Old Hinks had kept his occupation of Public Executioner a secret, which was not unnatural. In between his professional engagements he lived frugally, carrying on his business of cobbler. The sons seemed to have been aware of his sideline, for they had apparently both changed their name. During his career Hinks had been concerned with twenty-six hangings, and Lowe read through the list in the hope that it might suggest something. But his hope was in vain. It was possible that amongst these dead criminals was one whose family had taken vengeance against the family of the man who had been responsible for carrying out the sentence of death which had been imposed upon him. But there was no indication of which, and it would mean an endless search with, quite possibly, negative results.

Apart from which Lowe was a little sceptical of the vengeance theory. It seemed hardly likely. But what other was there? Old Hinks had died ten years previously of chronic alcoholic poisoning, predeceased by his wife a matter of two years. One son had been killed in the war, the other was Hammond. There was no mention of any other relatives. The only possibility if gain was behind the murders at Backwaters, was that this man John Hinks was responsible, that he had not been killed in the war.

This was a feasible supposition. Countless people had been reported 'missing' only to appear again after an interval of time. There was nothing against that. But who was he? Certainly no one Lowe had yet met.

He laid aside the papers concerning the brief account of Hinks' history and slowly filled and lit his pipe. He was annoyed and irritable.

It looked very much as if he would have to admit defeat and acknowledge that for once he was beaten. There was nothing to work on, no line of inquiry that could be followed with any hope of discovering the truth.

For the hundredth time he went over in his mind all the circumstances surrounding the three crimes, refreshing his memory from the notes which he had made previously. It was a thousand pities that he had not been more careful when he had the murderer within arm's reach in the lounge on that night when Mrs. Hammond had been killed. A thousand pities! He had had his chance then, and it had slipped through his fingers by sheer carelessness. Whoever was behind this business was cunning and clever. They had made no slip, no mistake, at least no noticeable mistake, and everybody's story had been tested where it was not confirmed by his own knowledge.

He cast his mind back to that Saturday afternoon, conjuring up a mental picture of the sequence of events. And suddenly he came upon something that had not been tested, unless Cotter had confirmed it.

It seemed quite unimportant, but at the same time —

He rose to his feet, crossed to the telephone directory, looked up the number of Bray Police Station, and put through a call. He was lucky. Cotter was in his office.

'Hello, Mr. Lowe!' he greeted when he came to the phone. 'I hope you've got some good news for me, I can do with some.'

'I'm afraid I haven't,' said the dramatist. 'But I've got a question to ask you.' He put it briefly.

'No,' answered the inspector. 'I didn't. I didn't think there was any need. What's the point?'

'I don't know that there's any point at all,' answered Lowe. 'Since the statement, however, has never been confirmed we can't take it as a fact.'

'It was an error on my part,' said the inspector. 'But it can easily be rectified. I'll check it and let you know.'

'Do,' said Lowe, and hung up the receiver.

He went back to the chair and his thoughts. It was twenty minutes later when Cotter rang back, and the excitement in his voice was clearly audible.

'I've checked that, Mr. Lowe,' he said. 'It was a he!'

'You're sure of that?' asked the dramatist quickly, and his eyes narrowed.

'Absolutely!' declared the inspector. 'There's no doubt whatever.'

'Cotter,' said Lowe, 'there's an old saying that every criminal, however clever he is, makes one slip. I think we've found it.'

'But — good Lord! Who would have thought — '

'I'm coming down,' said Lowe. 'I'll be with you in about an hour and a half.'

* * *

Trevor Lowe and Inspector Cotter faced each other across the latter's desk in his tiny office at the police station.

'Just one little lie!' said the dramatist softly. 'And an unnecessary lie, too. What a fool!'

'It's not enough proof to warrant an arrest,' said Cotter dubiously.

'No. But now we know the person,' retorted Lowe, 'the proof will possibly be easier to find.'

'Do we know the person?' muttered the inspector. 'Aren't you taking rather a lot for granted, Mr. Lowe?'

'I'm taking nothing for granted,' said the dramatist. 'Can you give me any plausible reason for that lie, other than a guilty one?'

'Well, no, I can't,' said Cotter candidly, after a pause. 'And when you come to look at it like that it seems pretty conclusive. But it wouldn't be conclusive enough to go before a jury.'

'I'm aware of that,' said Lowe. 'How many murderers are walking about today who are known to the police to be guilty, and cannot be arrested because of insufficient evidence to go before a jury?'

'Yes, that's true,' said the inspector. 'What we lack in this case is a motive.'

'I think that can be found,' said the dramatist quietly. 'I've made one or two discoveries since I saw you last, Cotter, and when you hear one of them I think you'll agree with me that the motive should not be difficult to guess.'

He related all that he had learned, and Cotter listened, an expression of interest on his shrewd face.

'You've certainly been busy, sir,' he remarked, when the dramatist had finished. 'I suppose what you're suggesting is that John Hinks is still alive?'

'Yes, I'm suggesting just that,' said the dramatist.

'It's an extraordinary business,' said Cotter. 'Fancy Mr. Hammond being the son of old Hinks the Hangman. Incredible!'

'I presume hangmen have had sons before and will have them again,' said Lowe. 'There's really nothing incredible about it. It's only incredible in the light of the circumstances attaching to it.'

'Well, what do you suggest we do?' inquired the practical inspector. 'I don't mind admitting that I shall be very glad to bring this case to a conclusion, Mr. Lowe. As I think I told you, the Chief Constable has been agitating to call in the help of the Yard, and I've had all my work cut out to stop it. I suppose really it ought to have been done in the first place. But it'll mean a lot to me if I can bring this off on my own, and I didn't want the Yard to get the kudos.'

'Well, I think you stand a very good chance,' said the dramatist. 'After all, officially I'm only a private individual. Therefore any help I may be able to give you needn't be mentioned.'

'That's very kind of you,' said Cotter gratefully, 'and I appreciate it. How do you propose to set about getting the proof that we require?'

'Hard work and a modicum of luck!' answered Lowe. 'Which, incidentally, is a very good formula for success in anything.'

26

Reconstruction

During the ensuing week Lowe certainly carried out the first part of his formula, while the patient and bored detectives continued to keep the people who had been at Backwaters under observation. He was here, there, and everywhere. He interviewed officials at the War Office, took long journeys into the Midlands, probing, questioning, checking and tracing back the history of the man whose single slip had directed suspicion toward him.

But the second part of his formula — the modicum of luck that he had mentioned — failed to put in an appearance. It was true he made one or two minor discoveries, but none that offered any likelihood of supplying the proof which he and the police so urgently needed before they could take action.

He came back to Portland Place on the sixth day, a tired, irritable, and depressed man, with next to nothing to show for his labours.

His investigations had led him to a certain point, and from thence onwards he found himself up against a blank wall. Neither had Cotter been any more successful.

'It looks to me, Mr. Lowe,' he said gloomily, during an interview with the dramatist, 'as though we're going to fail for lack of evidence. If you're right, and I personally think you are, this fellow, except for that one mistake, has been infernally clever. He's covered his tracks so completely that we've got absolutely nothing against him except suspicion. And you know as well as I do that we can't act on that alone.'

'We could,' said Lowe, 'but it wouldn't do any good, and the first hint he got that we suspected him would spoil any chance we may yet have of fastening the guilt on him. There is, I think a forlorn hope, and if you're agreeable I'm prepared to take it.'

'What's that?' asked the inspector.

'To surprise him into an admission of

some sort,' replied the dramatist. 'Listen. Suppose we arrange to hold a reconstruction of Venita Shayne's murder. Invite everybody who was present at Backwaters on that Saturday to come down and go over the incidents from lunchtime onwards exactly as they took place on the day the girl was killed.'

Cotter looked dubious.

'I don't see what good that's going to do,' he remarked. 'This fellow's hardly likely to give himself away.'

'I'm not so sure,' said Lowe. 'Look at it from his point of view. At the moment he's under the impression that he's perfectly safe. He doesn't know that we've discovered the lie he told. Now, if we go through that reconstruction and suddenly disclose our knowledge the shock may force him into saying or doing something that will give him away. He won't have time to think because he won't expect his statement to be challenged. D'you see what I mean?'

'Yes, I see.' The inspector was still sceptical. 'It's rather an unusual proceeding, Mr. Lowe.'

The dramatist made an impatient gesture.

'Possibly it is! But we're dealing with an unusual situation!' he retorted. 'In my opinion it's the only way and there's no harm in trying it. I'm prepared to take full responsibility for the idea.'

Cotter was reluctant to agree, but after a certain amount of argument he grudgingly gave his consent.

On the following morning, which was a Friday, all the people who had been guests at Backwaters during that fatal weekend received a letter requesting them to come to the riverside house at midday on the Saturday. The letter was an official one, and although couched courteously admitted of no refusal.

With Minter's assistance the servants had been traced and also 'invited' to be present. Eric Norman called on the dramatist on the Friday evening.

'What's the idea of this?' he demanded, producing the letter he had received.

'The idea,' explained Lowe, 'is to reconstruct as far as possible, the circumstances surrounding the death of Miss Shayne.

The Police and I have an idea that by doing so we may be assisted to a solution of the mystery.'

The press agent was not enthusiastic.

'It'll be rather a gruesome proceeding,' he remarked.

'I don't imagine for one moment,' retorted Lowe, 'it's going to be a picnic! But I'm hoping the result will justify the rather unusual procedure.'

He arrived at Backwaters on the Saturday morning early, accompanied by Arnold White, and was met by Minter.

'The cook and the housemaid have already arrived, sir,' said the servant. 'I had a great deal of difficulty in getting them to consent, but they're here. Perhaps you'd like to see them.'

Lowe interviewed the two rather frightened women, calmed their fears, and explained to them exactly what he wanted. They were to carry out as far as possible a repetition of their movements on the Saturday when Venita Shayne had come by her death. Everything, as far as possible, was to be duplicated.

'I dunno as I can remember what we

did,' said the maid.

'Well, try!' urged Lowe. 'Even if you can't remember the details try as near as you can to do what you did that day.'

At half past eleven Eric Norman arrived, looking a little worried and uneasy, and almost immediately after came Marjorie Lovelace and Harold Cavendish. Although Cavendish had not been actually present on the day of the murder he had been in the vicinity, and Lowe had therefore included him in his list.

John Moore was late. It was nearly a quarter-past twelve before he put in an appearance, excusing himself on the grounds that he had been rehearsing for a new show and had had difficulty in getting away.

The dramatist took them all into the lounge and explained the reason for their presence.

'I can't see what you hope to gain, Mr. Lowe,' said Harold Cavendish, when they had grasped the idea.

'I'm hoping,' said the dramatist, 'that by re-enacting everything that happened prior to, during, and after Venita Shayne's murder somebody will recollect some-thing that during the excitement they forgot to mention. We now, with the exception, of course, of Mr. Hammond, Mrs. Hammond and Venita Shayne herself, have everybody here who was here on the occasion of her murder. I want, from the finish of luncheon onwards, everybody, as far as possible, to do exactly what they did then, paying particular attention to where they were at certain times. I have here,' — he produced a paper — 'the main times, and we shall follow those as near as we can. My secretary will take the place of Miss Shayne. I will take the place of Montague Hammond, and Inspector Cotter, for the occasion, will enact the role of Mrs. Hammond. So far as you're able I should like you even to remember what you said at the time. It will all help to lend reality to the atmosphere, and that's what I'm most anxious to obtain.'

The faces before him were troubled and uneasy. It was obvious that none of them had any relish for the situation.

'Sounds a lot of nonsense to me,'

muttered John Moore sullenly. 'Just a waste of time.'

'You may quite possibly be right, Mr. Moore,' said Lowe coldly. 'On the other hand you may not! It is only after we have reached the end of this experiment we shall know. Now, you all understand exactly what is required, don't you? I want you to imagine that this is the Saturday on which Venita Shayne was murdered. I want you to think back to that afternoon and try to remember everything that happened. By *everything* I mean any occurrence, no matter how trivial or apparently unimportant, that may have left an impression on your memory, or anything you may have forgotten at the time but which this reconstruction of the circumstances may bring back to your mind. Now luncheon will be served on the terrace exactly as it was on that day, and it will be served in ten minutes. From that time onwards I want everybody to behave as nearly as they can in conformity with their behaviour on the Saturday I mentioned.'

They were nervous. They looked at

each other covertly, and from each other to Lowe and the inspector. When Minter announced lunch and they took their seats at the table, occupying the same places as they had done before, their nervousness increased. There was a tension in the atmosphere, an excitement that was noticeable in a thousand trivial matters. Even Lowe felt it. His pulse was beating a little quickly, and when White brought up the subject of the watch, using the very words that Venita Shayne had used that fatal afternoon, there was a soft sigh of pent-up breath.

At another time there might have been an element of humour in the secretary enacting the role of the girl, but everybody was too keyed up, too expectant, too fearful, to notice anything funny in the situation.

It was surprising, Lowe thought, watching, how nearly this luncheon coincided with that other.

In spite of their obvious uneasiness they played up to the idea manfully. Their conversation was, with very little exception, a repetition of that other conversation, the conversation which had been the prelude to the tragedy.

When the meal was over and Arnold, as Venita Shayne had done, rose with the remark that he had some letters to write, Lowe replied in the words of Hammond 'that he could use the study'. Cotter, primed, suggested bridge as Mrs. Hammond had done on that fatal day. Marjorie Lovelace, John Moore, and Lowe, in his character of Hammond, agreed.

'You can count me out,' said Norman. 'I loathe the game and I'm a bad player. I'm in the middle of a rattling good thriller and I want to finish it.'

As he had done before, he accompanied White into the house, and Lowe went with them.

'Do exactly what you did before,' he murmured, as they passed Minter with a card table, which he was carrying out from the lounge.

Norman, at Arnold's side, went up the stairs. At the door of the study he paused.

'See you when you've finished your letters,' he remarked, and White, nodding, opened the door and disappeared.

Norman continued on his way down the corridor, entering the room that he had occupied previously at the far end. After a little while he returned.

'I should be carrying a book,' he said.

'All right,' said Lowe. 'That doesn't matter. Go on.'

The press agent went leisurely down the stairs, passed through the lounge and out down the steps of the terrace to the lawn. The others were grouped round the bridge table.

Minter met Lowe as he returned to the house.

'Now what did you do?' said the dramatist.

'I went up to my room, sir,' answered the servant.

Lowe looked at his watch. It was exactly two twenty-five.

'Carry on,' he said.

Minter went out into the hall and ascended the stairs, disappearing round the bend. Lowe waited. At two-thirty-one Minter came down, and hovered about the hall for a moment, and then went through to the servants' quarters. Lowe glanced at Cotter.

'So far so good,' he murmured.

The inspector, a worried frown on his face, nodded.

'Yes,' he replied. 'But the crucial moment's coming.'

'According to the evidence of the burn,' remarked Lowe, 'Venita Shayne is now dead.' He exhibited the dial of his watch. It was two-thirty-nine.

They waited in silence. Just before three Minter reappeared through the door leading to the kitchen and began to straighten the ornaments in the hall.

'Milly, the housemaid, sir,' he remarked, 'has gone down to the gate, as she did, if you remember, before.'

Lowe nodded. His nerves were tense and he had all he could do to control his excitement. Was this experiment of his going to be successful or not? The next hour would show.

Leaving Cotter in the hall he strolled through the lounge and surveyed the people on the lawn. They were pretending to play bridge.

The chair that he himself had occupied

on that Saturday was in the same position. White had been on the river. Eric Norman was sitting where he had sat before, the only difference being that this time he was not reading.

Ten minutes past three . . . a quarter past three . . . twenty past three.

Lowe returned to the hall. Minter was standing near the front door, glancing out through one of the glass panels. Inspector Cotter sat on a hard chair, tense and expectant. The grandfather clock showed three-twenty-five . . . three-thirty.

Minter swung round listening intently.

'This,' murmured Lowe, 'was when you heard the telephone bell?'

The servant nodded.

'Yes, sir,' he answered. 'It rang. And then it rang again. I waited, and when it rang a third time I hurried upstairs.' He acted to suit the words, disappearing round a bend in the staircase. Lowe exchanged a glance with Cotter. Presently he came down, hurriedly, jerkily, his face drawn. Without taking any notice of the two men who were watching him he hurried through the lounge, across the terrace and down on to the lawn. Lowe following saw him talking agitatedly to the group at the card table, saw them get up, saw them follow him across the lawn, up the steps into the lounge to the hall. Minter had one foot on the staircase when the dramatist's voice cut sharply into the proceedings.

'Stop!' he said curtly. 'There's no need to go any farther!'

They halted, faces white and strained, figures tense with expectant, taut muscles.

'You've all done exactly as you did that other Saturday? You've made no mistake, no difference?'

A concerted shaking of heads answered him.

'You, Minter? You heard the telephone bell, expected Miss Shayne to answer it and when she didn't went up and found her — dead?'

The servant nodded.

'You picked up the receiver and found it was a wrong number. Rushed down to inform your master of your horrible discovery?'

'Yes, sir,' said Minter.

'You lie!' thundered Lowe. 'You lied then and you're lying now, John Hinks! There was no telephone bell to call you to the study that afternoon! No call was put through to this number from the exchange during the whole of Saturday. It was the one slip you made and it's going to hang you!'

27

The Killer!

Minter's lips curled back in a snarl of hate and fury and his hand flew to the hip pocket of his sombre grey trousers, but the watchful Cotter was too quick for him. With one spring the inspector covered the distance between them and gripped the man's wrist just as he was withdrawing the weapon.

'Oh, no, you don't!' he snapped, and gave Minter's arm a vicious twist.

The tiny automatic fell with a clatter to the polished floor, and Lowe heaved an inward sigh of relief. His bluff had come off! As he had hoped the man had given himself away. The suddenness of the accusation had taken him by surprise — the suddenness and the realisation that his lie had been discovered.

'How did you know?' he muttered. 'How did you know?'

'I didn't, but I know now!' retorted the dramatist coolly. 'You killed Venita Shayne, Mrs. Hammond, and your brother!'

There was a gasp from the others and he saw consternation and surprise on the faces round him.

'Do you — do you mean that this fellow is Montague Hammond's brother?' stammered Eric Norman incredulously.

'I do!' declared Lowe. 'His name is John Hinks, and he and Montague Hammond are the sons of Charles Hinks, the Public Executioner.'

The surprise evoked by his last statement was nothing to that created by this.

'Public Executioner?' squeaked John Moore. 'My God!'

'You can't prove it!' snarled Minter.

'We've no need to!' snapped Lowe. 'All we've got to prove is that you killed Venita Shayne, and on that you've given yourself away. You were clever, but you made one mistake. You told a lie, a lie that wasn't really necessary. You said the reason that had caused you to make the discovery was hearing the telephone. You never heard the telephone for the simple reason that the telephone bell never rang. Inspector Cotter has checked up at the exchange and no call was put through to here that Saturday, and they remember this particularly because Montague Hammond had queried his last account and a special watch was kept on all calls emanating from and arriving at Backwaters. There was no reason for the lie except to make a plausible excuse for your discovery.'

Minter glared at him and a little dribble of saliva flecked his thin lips.

'You — you — ' he began incoherently, almost choking in his rage, and then burst into a flood of foul invectives.

'That'll do!' snapped Lowe sharply. 'Take him away, Cotter!'

The inspector, who had never let go his grip, began the usual formula, but Minter turned on him with a face like the face of a wild beast.

'Let me go!' he shouted. 'Let me go, curse you! So you set a trap for me, did you, you cunning devil! But I'll beat you yet. You've got no proof. No proof at all.'

'That 'ull do!' cried Cotter angrily. 'We don't want any more from you!'

But the man was struggling violently, shouting and raving and screaming, and Lowe had to go to the inspector's assistance. And even with his help it was all they could do to drag him away. Eventually, however, Cotter succeeded in handcuffing his wrist and handing him over to the tender mercies of the sergeant and a gaping constable whom he had brought for just such an emergency.

'And that's that!' remarked the dramatist quietly. 'I congratulate you, Cotter, on having brought the case to a successful conclusion.'

The inspector made a grimace.

'I'd never have dared to do what you did, Mr. Lowe,' he answered. 'If you'd been wrong there'd have been the devil to pay.'

'I wasn't wrong,' said Trevor Lowe complacently. 'And after all, when you're up against it you've got to take a chance.'

★　★　★

It was several days later before the whole truth came out, and it is doubtful if this would ever have been satisfactorily proved if Minter, or, to give him his real name, John Hinks, hadn't made a full confession.

Although there was nothing to implicate him in the murder of Montague Hammond and Mrs. Hammond, his guilt concerning the death of Venita Shayne was unquestionable. Realising this, he made a clean breast of the whole business. Lowe was present when he made his statement, and related the gist of it later to the interested Arnold White.

'Apparently,' he said, 'before he joined the Army Hinks had got into some sort of trouble. He had a job as accountancy clerk with a Lancashire iron works, and he'd embezzled a certain amount of money, not a very large sum, but more than he could put back. This had been one of his main reasons for enlisting. The owners of the foundry, when they heard he'd joined the Army, took no further action, which was very decent of them. But Hinks didn't know this, and when he was posted 'missing' he saw a good opportunity of evading the arrest that he imagined was waiting for him when he came back.

'He exchanged his identity disc and papers with a dead comrade, deserted, and managed to keep himself hidden until the armistice was declared and the war was over. Then he took the name of Minter and lived precariously, doing a job here and a job there, until eventually he succeeded in obtaining a post as footman with Lord Deal. Here he remained for some time, falling in love with and marrying the under-housemaid. He had lost all touch with his family and had no reason for renewing it. His father was a poor man and he had no wish to be known as a relation of the Public Executioner.

'His brother seemed to have disappeared completely. And then by accident he recognised him in the person of Montague Hammond.

'Lord Deal had sent him to the theatre to book seats for one of Hammond's first nights, and while he was standing by the box office in the foyer he saw the producer. He had altered a little and aged, but he recognised him. Hammond was totally unaware that the soberly clad servant whom he passed was the brother who was supposed to have lost his life in the war, but the meeting and recognition on the part of John had started an idea in his brain.

'His brother was a wealthy man and he was poor, an under-servant getting a microscopic wage and living a life of drudgery. How could he lay hands on some of his brother's wealth?

'His first idea had been to reveal his identity and trust to the generosity of his brother, but he discarded this on second thoughts. He might squeeze a few pounds out of him that way, but not more. He made careful and secret inquiries, discovered that his brother was living in a house by the river and that he was married and had no children, and laid his plans.

'At this period he had no idea that Venita Shayne was his niece.

'He heard that Hammond was in search of a butler, applied for the job, and got it. And then he learned what was later to prove the genesis of his scheme of murder.

'He overheard a conversation between Venita Shayne and Hammond which revealed the relationship between them. The girl was demanding that certain debts that she had contracted should be paid off. Hammond gave her a bearer cheque for a hundred and fifty pounds and mentioned at the same time that he had made a will leaving her half his fortune, the other half to go to his wife.

'From that moment his brother decided to eliminate the three of them and claim the money for himself. He laid his plans carefully, waiting his opportunity. To confuse the issue he began sending Hammond anonymous letters containing abuse and threats and signed with the crude drawing of the dangling man, which he knew would lead Hammond to believe that the sender was aware of his real identity. His idea was to divert as much as possible suspicion from himself when the time came for the actual murder.

'When he heard Venita Shayne saying that her watch had stopped it gave him the idea of further confusing the issue by making the time of his premeditated crime appear later than it had actually taken place. When Venita Shayne announced her intention of writing letters and Hammond suggested she should use the study, he slipped up, altered the clock, came down again, and attended to the bridge table, as we saw.

'When he returned after that to the house he went straight to the study. Venita Shayne had begun her letter, timing it according to the clock before her. She took no notice, naturally, of Minter's entrance, beyond glancing up to see who it was, and he was able to pick up the statuette, stun her, and strangle her. As soon as she was dead he put the clock back to the right time and came down to the hall. The only mistake he made then was when he said he had heard a non-existent telephone call which had caused him to make the discovery.

'It was necessary he should make the discovery, since it helped to throw suspicion away from himself.

'Now only two people remained between him and a fortune, Hammond and Mrs. Hammond. He had decided on the order in which they were to be killed so as to further divert suspicion from the real motive.

'The murder of Hammond was his most cunning plan. He had decided that the two of them were to be killed during that weekend, and in preparation for the Hammond murder concealed on the island previously a powerful air gun. He underdressed on the Sunday morning with a bathing costume, slipped away after his duties, stripped, and swam to the island. He knew that on a fine morning Hammond was almost certain to be on the lawn. He shot him, as you know, just as Hammond was about to reveal to me whom he thought was the sender of the anonymous letters. I'm convinced that Hammond was under the impression that his wife had sent them. I don't think for one moment he had any suspicion as to the real sender.

'He shot Hammond, dropped the gun in the river, swam back, and redressed. He had ample time while I was occupied in a futile search of the island.

'Now there only remained Mrs. Hammond, and here he again evinced ingenuity. Mrs. Hammond, in her jealousy, had stolen

Venita Shayne's diary in the hope that she would discover something in its contents to justify her suspicions concerning the relationship between the dead girl and her husband.

'When John Hinks killed her he wore nothing. He stripped himself naked for the crime to avoid any possibility of bloodstains on his clothing. That's why Cotter's search revealed nothing of the sort. He stabbed her and discovered the diary. Fearful that it might contain something he took it, carried it down to the lounge, and was examining it by the light of the candle when I interrupted him. He had to act swiftly and he did. He stunned me with a heavy bookend, before I was able to catch a glimpse of him. Then he returned to his room, washed off the stains of blood with which he was spattered and went to bed.

'He was up early on the following morning and had destroyed the diary in the furnace of the central heating plant before anyone was down.

'A clever, callous man, and he nearly achieved his object.'

Lowe paused to light his pipe.

'What I can't understand,' said White, 'is how he expected to get hold of the money without giving himself away?'

'He explained that,' said his employer. 'And it wasn't so difficult. He intended to slip abroad, dropping all trace of his identity as Minter. From one of the colonies he would have written to Hammond's solicitors disclosing his real identity and submitting conclusive proof, which he had in his possession. He would have proved that Montague Hammond was James Hinks and that he was John, who was supposed to have died in the war. He would have offered as an excuse for the fact that he had allowed his brother and other people to think this the plausible argument of his father's official capacity as Hangman and his very natural wish not to be associated in any way.'

'I wonder if he would have got away with it?' murmured the secretary.

'I think he would,' said Lowe. 'After all, there was no other claimant. He was the only surviving member of the family, so the question of contesting his claim would not arise. The police might have been suspicious if the matter had come to their ears, but it's doubtful if they could have offered sufficient proof to warrant an arrest any more than he would ever have been found out if he hadn't made that one stupid slip over the telephone call. That was his undoing, and even that would have been useless if the sudden shock of being accused had not led him to give himself away. Had he known it, he was in a very strong position. If he had only called my bluff, sworn that he thought he'd heard the telephone bell, I doubt if we could ever have brought the crimes home to him.

'There was nothing to connect him with John Hinks. He'd covered his tracks completely. I spent nearly a week trying to connect him with Hinks, and I failed. The majority of people who had known him in pre-war days were dead and no photographs of the original Hinks existed, except one which he had in his own possession and which he intended to use as one of the means of proving his identity when he made the claim.

'In reality, when you come to analyse it, the case was a very simple one. It was the side-issues that made it difficult, all the things that had no connection at all with the murders: the anonymous letters, the robbery at Venita Shayne's flat, the loss of the diary. All these combined to blind our eyes to the real and simple explanation.'

'I don't know that it was so simple,' grunted Arnold White. 'You might have suspected Minter of killing Venita Shayne if there'd been any motive for him to do so, but I'm hanged if anyone would ever have associated him with the murder of Hammond. I remember now, although I didn't mention it at the time, that I had some trouble in finding him to notify him of the murder. The other servants said he was upstairs somewhere, and I came to the natural conclusion. Of course what he was really doing was hurriedly redressing after swimming the river.'

'Yes, and everything more or less combined to act in his favour,' said Lowe. 'Cavendish coming to that island, Secket quarrelling with his wife and being in the vicinity.'

'I suppose,' said White, 'Minter sent her that letter?'

'Yes. Another of his ideas for confusing the issues,' said Lowe.

'He must have had a nerve,' remarked Arnold, 'to have carried out the second and third murders practically under the eyes of the police.'

'He had nerve enough in some respects,' agreed his employer. 'But his nerve failed him at the very moment when he needed it most.'

'It's a good job,' grinned White, 'that you're not officially connected with the police. If you had been you couldn't have done that, and this case would have gone down amongst the great 'unsolved crimes'.'

'I had a job,' said Lowe with a smile, 'to get Cotter to agree to the arrangement. He wasn't at all in favour with the reconstruction idea at first, but there you are. It was a risk, and it came off. If it hadn't come off I don't see that it would have done much harm. In the circumstances it was the only way to secure proof.'

'Well, you've got his confession now,'

said Arnold White. 'So the end justifies the means in any case.'

★ ★ ★

The newspapers made a feature of the apprehension of the Backwaters murderer and fulsome praise was lavished on Inspector Cotter for his remarkable achievement in solving the mystery. His photograph appeared on the front pages of nearly every journal, and the letter which he subsequently wrote to Trevor Lowe expressing his most grateful thanks for his assistance ended with a paragraph expressing his discomfort that he should have received so much praise when it was Lowe who had been really responsible.

The dramatist had, however, kept himself as much as possible in the background. He had no wish to steal Cotter's thunder. His satisfaction at having brought the difficult problem to a successful conclusion was sufficient reward. Therefore, although his name appeared in the newspapers it was in the minor capacity as having been present and he was referred to merely as an important witness.

The trial that took place in due course was one of the shortest known in criminal history. It lasted less than half an hour and the jury gave their verdict without retiring and the judge passed sentence.

The prisoner listened stolidly, maintaining a calm indifference, which had been a characteristic of his demeanour throughout the brief proceedings.

On a wet morning three weeks later a crowd gathered silently outside the dour and gloomy walls of Wandsworth Prison. A silent crowd who stood waiting as the hour of eight drew on. A clock began to strike and the heads of the men present were bared. There was an interval and then the wicket in the big gate opened. A uniformed official stepped through and pinned a sheet of paper to the notice board. The crowds pressed closer to get a view of the brief official announcement that John Hinks had paid the penalty for his crimes.

'Queer thing, ain't it,' said a stout woman, carrying a shopping basket. 'Son of Hinks the Executioner, 'e was. Now 'e's been 'anged 'isself. Queer! Like a book.'

'I've always said, Aggie,' said the man with her, 'that queerer things 'appen in real life than wot you see on the pitchers or read about in books.'

'Well, 'e deserved it,' said the woman. 'I saw that woman Venita Shayne once in a play. Lovely, she was. A pretty, childlike little thing, as she looked. 'E must have been a brute!'

'Maybe she wasn't so childlike as she looked,' grunted her husband. 'These flowery faced gals ain't always 'oney and cream. So I've been told,' he added hastily, as his wife looked sharply at him. Which piece of philosophy was nearer the truth than he imagined.

Marjorie Lovelace, dining quietly with Harold Cavendish, brought up the subject of the execution during the meal.

'I don't think,' she said with a little shiver, 'that I shall ever forget that weekend at Backwaters. It was the most terrible experience I've ever had. You were lucky. You never saw Venita after — afterwards.'

310

'No, I didn't,' he answered. 'But I'm afraid, Marjorie, I can't work up anything in the way of sympathy. I've told you what she was like, and you know a little also, from your own experience. I doubt if there's anyone who really and truly misses her.'

'It's a dreadful thing, but I believe you're right,' she answered. 'The only person who was really cut up when her death was discovered was Monty.'

'Well, he was her father, which is a different matter,' said Cavendish. 'I suppose after all blood's thicker than water, and in spite of her unpleasant characteristics he was fond of her. I've only one reason to be grateful to her,' he continued after a pause. 'If it hadn't been for her I should never have met you.'

'And you think that's important?' she murmured.

'I think it's the most important thing in the world!' he declared, and the remainder of the conversation was neither original nor interesting — except to the two people whom it concerned.

The summer had merged into autumn and Trevor Lowe, busy with other matters, had almost forgotten the strange business at Backwaters, when he was reminded of it one day as he and Arnold White were walking through the park for a short stroll before tea.

An enormous cream and red car passed them, slowed, drew into the sidewalk, and stopped. A man's head was thrust out of the window and a hand beckoned them peremptorily.

'Good Lord, who's that?' exclaimed the secretary in surprise. 'Must be a millionaire at least. What a dazzling contraption!'

'I think,' murmured Lowe, 'it's an old friend of ours.'

'An old — ' began Arnold, and broke off with a gasp as he recognised the face that was beaming at them.

It was Mr. Secket!

''Ow d'you do?' said that gentleman affably. ''Ow are yer?'

'We're very well, thank you,' remarked Lowe, and eyed the sumptuous machine

312

with slightly raised eyebrows.

'What d'yer think of 'er?' said Mr. Secket proudly. 'Beauty, ain't she? Care to come for a spin?'

The dramatist shook his head.

'No, thank you,' he answered. 'We're just going home.'

'Drop you, if you like,' said the genial little man. 'Goin' that way meself. Got to call in at the office to sign me letters.'

'Are you in business then, now?' asked Lowe.

Mr. Secket dived a beringed hand into the inner pocket of his check suiting, produced a dazzling wallet, and took out a card.

'There y'are,' he said proudly. 'Come and see me any time you like, mister.'

Lowe examined the gold-edged card, which bore in flowing script:

Secket's Vaudeville and
Variety Agency.'
Alkazar House, W.C.1

'I hope you're doing well,' he remarked.
'Very well, thank you,' said Mr. Secket.

'It's an ill wind that blows nobody no good. Well, if you won't come, you won't, and I must be off. Goodbye and good luck. Get going, Charlie,' he said to the stolid chauffeur, and the car moved off.

Trevor Lowe gazed after it silently.

'Penny for 'em,' said Arnold White, breaking in on his thoughts.

He started and shrugged his shoulders.

'I was just thinking what a queer world it is,' he murmured. 'Come on, or we'll be late for tea.'

THE END